"You may not always understand His ways, Charlotte, but He will not leave you comfortless or alone."

"That will be enough reading for now." Charlotte replaced the book and rose to take her candle that was now burning low.

"Don't leave yet," he said. "Tell me, Charlotte, what is it you spend your time reading and copying in the library?"

"Scripture verses, sir."

"Nothing else?"

"No, sir."

"I heard Wesley the last time he was in Lynnhampton but he made me very uncomfortable."

"It's a matter of asking God for forgiveness, sir, and you will find that your uncomfortable feelings will turn into feelings of peace. Only in Christ is there peace."

"You make it sound so simple," he stated flatly.

"It is, sir."

"No, Charlotte. In my case it's not that simple."

By now Charlotte's candle was so low that the wick burned out. She knelt by the fire to light what was left of it, but Mr. Tellison interrupted her. "Allow me," he said reaching for a fresh candle on the mantlepiece. When it burned brightly, he handed it to her.

THE CONVICTION OF CHARLOTTE GREY

Jeanne Cheyney

Serenade/Saga
BOOKS

of the Zondervan Publishing House
Grand Rapids, Michigan

A Note From The Author:

I love to hear from my readers! You may correspond with me by writing:

> Jeanne Cheyney
> 1415 Lake Drive S.E.
> Grand Rapids, MI 49506

The Conviction of Charlotte Grey
Copyright © 1985 by The Zondervan Corporation
Grand Rapids, Michigan

Serenade/Saga is an imprint of Zondervan Publishing House,
1415 Lake Drive, S.E., Grand Rapids, Michigan 49506.

Library of Congress Cataloging in Publication Data

ISBN 0-310-47182-6

Edited by Pamela M. Jewell
Designed by Kim Koning

Printed in the United States of America

85 86 87 88 89 90 91 / 10 9 8 7 6 5 4 3 2 1

CHAPTER 1

England, 1770

CHARLOTTE STARED INTO the flames but adamantly refused to move nearer to the fire. Instead, she pulled her cloak tightly about her to ward off the chilling, apprehensive feeling that crept in around her. No longer did a fire hold a silent fascination as it once did, for after it claimed her home and family, it filled her dreams with screaming, writhing horrors. Charlotte wondered if she would ever forget.

The circuit preacher brought in tea and sat beside her for a few moments. "We want you to stay with us, Charlotte. You know that, don't you?"

The girl shook her wheat-colored curls, but she had made up her mind. The preacher had barely enough essentials for his own family without the added burden of feeding her. No. She was healthy and knew how to manage and she would get along somehow— somewhere—with God's help. "I need employment," she said simply. Then her head rose and her lips formed a thin determined line.

7

She knew what the man was thinking when he studied her in the light from the fire. He had known her father, and known also, that he was a man of wealth who had given his three daughters fine clothes and tutors in the classics and the arts. They had had all the advantages that the lord of the castle enjoyed. "Everything was lost in that fire, sir. Except me," she whispered.

"Have you relatives who can provide a home for you, Charlotte?"

"No, sir. There is one uncle in Essex but he has had nothing to do with us since we became Christians. To him, we are heretics."

"Have you spoken to the steward at the castle?"

"Yes, sir, but there is no work of any kind there either," she said softly. Charlotte gnawed at her lower lip. Everyone in the village knew the castle had fallen deeply into debt from the young lord's gambling bouts. But, even so, the steward paid her well for her carriage and horses after she begged him to take them, for she couldn't bear to think of the animals suffering beatings or mistreatment by strangers. She felt the weight of those shillings tucked in her bosom. They were the sole possessions bridging the gulf between herself and starvation.

"Then we will be praying for you each day. Remember to trust God fully. You may not always understand His ways, Charlotte, but He will not leave you comfortless, or alone."

"I'll not forget," she whispered. Charlotte adjusted her cloak for departure while the man rose to accompany her to the gate. Then with her head held high, she walked on. Not once did she turn to the right or to the left as she traveled past the forge, the mill, the village cottages, or the pitiful charred remains of her home and family. With one purpose in mind, she moved onto the post road that led to the market town several miles beyond. She knew what she had to do.

The three miles of dusty, gorse-laced road that twisted from the village of Withanham to the nearest town was thronged with a cross section of society. They proceeded at various gaits on foot, in wagons, and carriages—all in the direction of Linton.

For only a few moments, Charlotte halted and turned her head back toward the village shrouded in morning mist and wondered if she would ever see Withanham again. While the chill air snatched at the tears that trickled from her eyes, she stumbled slightly and endeavored to check the muffled sobs held tightly within her breast.

She pushed herself along with the stream of travelers. At times she moved ahead, at others she lagged behind, but constantly Charlotte kept beyond the taunts and jeers of a few low-breds demanding attention with their filthy talk.

The late September morning had a chill in the air. For miles in all directions, the trees were beginning to exchange their summer greenery for more somber hues of autumn. Overhead, flocks of migrant birds flew in erratic loose maneuvers in preparation for southern flights. Before long, it would turn cold.

Just beyond the final bend in the post road, Charlotte saw the cathedral spires of Linton pointing skyward. The fair sprawled along one side of the boundaries. Her heart, by now, began pounding within her breast until it wracked her whole body of normal breath. Never had she thought her life would come to this.

With difficulty, Charlotte approached and pressed through the throngs in search of the employment line. From every direction came shouts and revelings. She tried first one alley and then another—past rows of cheeses, gingerbread, garlic, and sweets. Hucksters screamed into her ears. They offered their fresh fruits, aniseed, gin, and oysters while rotten smells of fish drifted from some nondescript booth nearby. Charlotte stumbled forward to keep from retching.

As she crossed the main thoroughfare, a lively fiddler gave his sunken, toothless grin to passersby. He endeavored to lure customers into low booths smelling of gin and ringing with filthy curses. Everywhere people parted willingly with hard earned pence for frivolous baubles and trappings—pence that should have gone for necessities.

Charlotte tore herself loose from the disgusting scene about her and ran, weary and exhausted, to the far end of the fair grounds. A line of men, women, and children of all ages were being viewed and questioned by a random gathering of well dressed gentlemen and farmers. Each wore a sign of his trade. Charlotte stood for a moment to collect her thoughts before she walked across the opening and took her place in the line.

The two women standing beside her studied her for a moment, then one sneered. "Them's mighty fine clothes you be wearing, Miss. Where did you get 'em, eh, girlie? Some young buck give 'em fer favors?" And the creature leaned forward, jabbed Charlotte sharply in the ribs with her elbow, and winked at the woman by her side.

Charlotte sickened and tried in vain to keep her eyes straight ahead. But she became more and more agitated with the woman's taunts and handling until she finally moved, in desperation, to another place in line. At that same moment, a gentleman came and stood directly in front of her. He studied her face and then allowed his eyes to run down the full length of her body while Charlotte lowered her eyes to hide her embarrassment. The lines of his mouth moved in a motion of contemplation while his hands stayed clasped behind him. She knew she was an unusual sight with clothes that were too finely made for a gathering such as this.

"Tell me," he said looking directly into her eyes, "since you apparently have not chosen to wear a symbol of your trade, just what *is* your trade, Miss?"

Charlotte stood for one horrified moment then quickly composed herself and looked directly into the dark eyes of the young gentleman before her. "Housekeeper, sir," she said clearly.

The young man continued to study her. "How old are you?"

"Twenty one, sir."

"And you were a housekeeper before you came here today?"

"Yes. I helped manage my father's house."

"And he fired you, apparently." The gentleman by now was openly amused. A second man stood somewhat to the rear.

"Well, Shannon, what do you think? Would she make Mrs. Tellison a good housekeeper?" He turned to the man standing behind him and waited for an answer.

"Clean and comely enough, sir, if she can perform her duties as she says."

"Yes. Yes, you are right." Then turning back to the young woman he asked, "Can you cook?"

"Very well, sir." she answered softly.

"Bake, mend, and clean?"

"Yes."

"Well, then, we shall make a bargain, Miss— Miss—"

"Grey. Charlotte Grey," answered the girl numbly.

He reached into his pocket for a luck-penny to make it a binding agreement, then spoke to the young woman facing him. "Now come along and we shall see just how much your word is worth." He motioned impatiently to the man at his side and ordered, "Shannon, get us some food for I am absolutely starved. We'll meet you at the carriage."

11

It took nearly a running pace to follow closely at the heels of Mr. Tellison as he followed around the fringes of the fair. Now that she had a token of security with another human being, Charlotte didn't intend to get separated from him. He was a tall, well-built man of thirty four, with thick chestnut hair pulled back and tied. His slender height was clothed in nicely fitted waistcoat, breeches and white stockings. That he was handsome, there was no doubting. In Charlotte's thinking, he had a definite air of importance about him and she wondered what he did for a living.

The gentleman moved steadily along. Not once did he turn to make sure that his newly bound servant followed as a trained hound at his heels until he approached a well equipped carriage.

"Shannon is in the process of buying us food, Samuel. And this," he partially turned to motion toward the young woman who was unquestionably behind him, "is Mrs. Tellison's new housekeeper, Miss Grey." The gentleman held his position and stared directly into the girl's face for a moment of intense study. Samuel looked at Charlotte with suppressed shock, but recovered his dignity sufficiently to nod and greet her with a civil, "Pleased, Miss," before returning to the business at hand.

Charlotte's weariness, by now, was apparent to Mr. Tellison for he said, "Samuel, Miss Grey would like to be seated." And the man obediently opened the carriage door and helped the girl enter. When she felt the weight of rich, gold velvet upholstery give beneath her body, she sank in complete exhaustion and leaned her head back against the seat.

It was some time before Shannon made his way back to the waiting carriage. His arms were precariously maneuvering heaps of cheeses, oysters, and fruit. He passed the food around and Charlotte accepted her portion gratefully. But before she ate, she bowed her head and offered a silent prayer of thanksgiving for her employment before taking a bite of her food. If the men noticed, they said nothing. Each ate in mute silence, assessing the newest addition to the household with no show of emotion escaping their sober faces.

The journey from the Linton fair to the seaport town of Lynnhampton was a distance of five miles. Charlotte gazed with half closed eyes at the beauty passing by.

Her mind once again sifted through the hideous events of the past two days. Why did it have to be her father who was taken in that fire? With his generosity in giving, he did so much good for the Lord through Reverend John Wesley's chapel. And his life was exemplary. Mr. Wesley, himself, thanked God for the man's life and leadership among the followers. She *must* believe that God's will was in all of this misery that befell her, although she couldn't understand how—or why.

Charlotte was aware that Mr. Tellison sat opposite her and quietly discussed some matters of business with Mr. Shannon. Then he spent the remainder of the time reading documents that he carried with him. From time to time she was remotely aware that he peered beyond the tops of his papers at her slender frame sitting opposite him in the carriage. His jaw was square, his eyes and brows were dark, and his mouth rested in a firm set of determination. He casually slung one ankle over a knee. The picture he represented was one of mastering any situation that faced him, and she felt certain no one defied him, ever. When at last Mr. Tellison pushed his hat forward on his head, he slouched slightly in his seat. With closed eyes, he whispered to Mr. Shannon, "What will Mrs. Tellison say when she sees what I brought her?" And with this, a slight smile appeared at one corner of his mouth.

On the outskirts of Lynnhampton, the carriage made a sharp right turn to follow the main road through the seaport town and beyond. For about two miles they traveled until they approached a majestic stone edifice of towers, buttresses, and loggias resting in seclusion behind ancient, rose-covered walls, and balustrades. An avenue, directly before the approach to the main gates, was lined with towering elms. The trees cast nervous shadows from the afternoon sun on the roadway and carriage as it passed beneath their branches.

When the carriage came to a stop, Mr. Tellison hopped out lightly and entered the house at the front entrance. Charlotte and the two men continued on to the rear.

What will Mrs. Tellison be like? she wondered to herself. Will she be pretty, even-tempered, stern, or passive? And her courage nearly failed her when she fully contemplated her duties within the proportions of this manor. The well ordered house of her father, with its staff of six servants, was in no way comparable to this magnificent country estate.

For a moment she questioned whether she made the right decision in going to Linton at all, but she reminded herself that the only alternative was to overburden the circuit preacher's family. And *that* was out of the question.

When Charlotte was summoned to the library, she uttered a plea for God's help, for her mouth was dry and her achingly weary limbs shook. But she endeavored to hold her head high, advance forward, and place herself near Madam Tellison. She reminded herself that she was God's child and nothing could harm her.

The older woman moved her dark head to the side and looked directly into the girl's face. She studied Charlotte from head to foot with a direct, piercing scrutiny before speaking.

"I am Miss Grey, madam," Charlotte said calmly when the awkward silence was unbearable. For some moments the woman said nothing but continued to gaze at the slender girl standing before her. Then suddenly the woman's voice gave vent to a vehemently whispered oath.

Charlotte winced at the disrespectful use of her Savior's name, and tried to determine what the oath signified. What was the woman thinking?

"How old are you?" demanded Mrs. Tellison.

"Twenty one, madam."

The woman raised her head and once again stared at Charlotte with a churlish curling of the lip. "What," demanded the woman, "can you do?"

"I can manage a household as well as cook, sew, mend, and clean."

"You have a grand manner about you, Miss Grey," she said sternly, "Just when did you begin aping your betters?"

At this, Charlotte felt strong personal rebuke against her family and the suggested deception on her part. She suppressed the sudden anger rising in her and answered calmly, "My family was well to do, madam, and I have had many advantages of education."

"Then you read well? Sing and play?" The woman's eyes narrowed somewhat as she waited for the girl's response.

"Yes, madam."

After what seemed an eternity of contemplation, the woman turned her bulky frame to the window and said, "Please wait outside in the passage."

Charlotte walked to the door, opened it, and obediently seated herself on a chair beyond the library. She folded her hands in her lap and assessed the situation. Mrs. Tellison was a coarse woman who was much older than her husband. She was, Charlotte

15

guessed, in her middle forties. She was dowager in her build, with raven hair and eyes, and thick lips that formed a hard look in her round face. Possibly Mr. Tellison married her for her money. It was not an uncommon thing. But he didn't seem the type at all.

Mr. Tellison strode down the passage with the familiar rapid gait. He acknowledged Charlotte's presence with neither nod nor glance but went straight to the library. The door failed to latch properly and remained ajar. Charlotte didn't mean to eavesdrop, but the voices behind the wall were loud enough to be heard and she was well aware of what was said.

"What possessed you to bring this child to take care of my household?" said Mrs. Tellison spitting out the words.

"*My* household, madam," said the man. "It is mine. Remember?"

"How dare you!" she lashed at him.

Charlotte closed her eyes and pictured Mr. Tellison refusing to take his eyes from the woman's face. No love was involved in that union. That was certain.

"What can this girl of twenty one possibly know about managing housekeeping duties?"

"Madam, if you could have seen the alternatives, you would be less severe in your criticism of the situation, for I guarantee that she was the best of the crop."

"Very well. I have no choice for now, but I do not intend to keep her if she proves unfit."

"The bargain was for one year."

The voices grew quieter and Charlotte heard no more. She felt like crying. The events of the past two days were crushing enough without having to work for a woman who wanted her about as much as she wanted the plague on her head. "Lord," she breathed when she put her head back against the chair, "I've got to have the strength to get through all this. I can't go on without your help for I'll wither and die."

16

The next words were spoken near the doorway. "I'll have the seamstress make her a few gowns, for she brought no boxes."

Charlotte's eyes were studying her clasped fingers when the gentleman emerged from the library. She glanced up for a moment to study him. He wore the same calm expression as when he entered the room.

"Please go in, Miss Grey," he said without so much as a look in her direction. "And do something about fixing your hair."

"Yes, sir." But she wondered what, exactly, he wanted her to do with it.

When Mrs. Tellison condescended to turn and face Charlotte again, she asked sternly, "Why didn't you bring any boxes?"

"I had none to bring, madam. Everything I owned perished in the fire."

"And what was the cause of that fire?"

"A careless servant," whispered Charlotte.

"We tolerate no carelessness here." Then in somewhat subdued tones she added, "My seamstress will fit you for gowns." Charlotte nodded and continued to stand before the glowering gaze of the woman.

"Your wages were set by the Statutes and we intend to abide by them as long as your work proves satisfactory. Do you understand?"

"Yes, madam, I understand," Charlotte answered.

Mrs. Tellison pulled a red cord and proceeded to talk. "Mr. Shannon is the steward. You will be directly responsible to him and all ordering must be approved by him."

From the library, Charlotte was led down a long, plain passage with stone floors laid in a pattern of black and white tiles. Very little ornamentation encumbered the hallway except a few chests shoved against the walls.

She struggled with her fears when she thought of

17

the woman's stern assessment and piercing eyes. When the heavy, oak door to her newly assigned apartment closed behind her, Charlotte leaned back against it for support. The feeling that overcame her began deep within. She laid on the bed and allowed herself to weep for the first time in two days. "Oh, God," she cried. "Be with me. Don't let me face this thing alone. Let me feel your presence as my Guide, my Comforter, my Strength," she pleaded. "I need Your help so desperately and I can't go on if You don't go with me. Take my hand in Yours," she sobbed. And even as she prayed, she felt a warmth, a sustaining, abiding glow, that reached deep into her soul and lifted her to a higher plane than she had known in days.

The following morning, Mr. Shannon introduced Charlotte to the staff of Tellison Hall and then carefully outlined the duties of each. He showed Charlotte the first floor and pointed out that the dinnerware and porcelains were of great value and needed special handling.

They continued to the second story to see both Mr. and Mrs. Tellison's apartment. The manor was of immense proportions and she was afraid that she would get lost a number of times before she had the layout clearly pictured in her mind. Charlotte secretly marveled at the great distance between the two chambers of the man and his wife. But that, of course, was none of her business. She thought that if Mr. Tellison were *her* husband she'd want to be as close as possible for he—" With this, she silently rebuked herself for such sinful thoughts concerning a married man; a man who was the handsome husband of her mistress, and no concern of hers other than keeping the house in a satisfactory condition to please him.

When they descended once again to the first floor, the steward escorted Charlotte to the morning room where the account books and staff manuals were kept and written in many hands. They spent much time going over these accounts and documents. By early afternoon she was officially the housekeeper of Tellison Hall, and the responsibility of its welfare rested solely on her shoulders.

For the remainder of the afternoon, and into the night, Charlotte studied the account books to learn exactly how the household operated. She poured over amounts of food used, the prices, and where purchases were made, until her eyes refused to function properly and she stumbled exhausted to her room.

Beginning with that day, Charlotte was determined to keep her staff under control for she was sure that many tended toward slovenliness. "Time," her father once said, "is a gift of God and is to be used to the best of one's ability." And she felt that the wisdom of that statement would not hurt the workers of Tellison Hall. With God's help she would succeed.

CHAPTER 2

THE THIRD DAY AFTER THE FITTING, the seamstress came with one of the finished dresses. Charlotte was so eager for a gown to replace the only one she had, that she immediately went in to try it on. A mirror hung at the far end of her apartment, and without hesitation, she moved before it at an advantageous distance to study her reflection. When she viewed herself, she was stunned. "This gown is indecent," gasped Charlotte. "Surely the woman made a mistake in cutting it. What am I to do? I have no gauze to form a shawl." As she debated her predicament, the thought occurred to her that Bessie would have some scraps of cloth lying about—scraps that could be made into a small shawl to cover the exposed neck and shoulders.

Charlotte was so anxious to reach Bessie's apartment, that she didn't see Mr. Tellison approaching from the opposite direction until the two collided full force. His arms immediately went about her to keep her from falling. But instead of letting go of her when she was steady once more, he continued to keep his arms firmly about her. Charlotte struggled to be free of those entwining bonds, and in her efforts, her eyes inadvertently met his for just an instant. She thought her heart would stop its beating right there on the spot. Immediately, she rebuked herself for her shameless, irresponsible behavior, and with a renewed effort, pried loose with a stammered, "I—I'm truly sorry. Forgive me." And to hide her embarrassment, she put her hands to her face to gain her composure as best she could. The man stood directly before her, gazing first at her carefully curled light hair, and then down the entire length of her body. She could feel her face turn crimson.

"Would you please turn around?" he commanded.

"Sir?" Surely she hadn't heard the man correctly.

"Come. Do as I say. Turn around. More slowly, please," he said. She felt his eyes engulfing her, and she wished for a small crack in the tiles to swallow her. But none did, so she simply stood there feeling miserably awkward and foolish.

The side of Mr. Tellison's mouth raised into a rather pleased half smile. While she remained frozen to the spot, he commenced his journey around her, studying her from all sides. "Yes," he said, "she did a fine job." The man came to a standstill before her. Then just as impulsively as he had stopped, he turned and continued his rapid pace down the passage saying only, "Proceed, Miss Grey."

At this point, she drew her breath in with indignation and *did* proceed as commanded down the hallway. But she hoped that the ridiculous scene wasn't seen by either Madam Tellison or the servants.

At Bessie's chamber, Charlotte knocked on the door. After entering, she approached the far end of the room where the woman sewed by the window. "How—how could you?" she demanded of the seamstress.

21

"Please sit down, ma'am," Bessie said calmly.

Charlotte shook her head and refused. "The dress—why?"

"I was carrying out orders, ma'am."

"Orders?" She was appalled at the statement. "From whom?"

"Mr. Tellison. He walked into my chamber the day you came. After looking through the available cloth, he selected the one that you are now wearing and the three that I am working on now. He also gave me specific instructions on how to put them together."

"I see," the girl said. "Isn't it rather unusual for the gentleman of the Hall to be so concerned with his servants' clothes?" By now Charlotte realized Bessie was not at fault and was sorry for her hasty accusations.

"Maybe. I know so few gentlemen."

"Perhaps you have a little gauze cloth that could be used as a small neck shawl?" she asked softly.

"It won't do any good, Ma'm."

"That may be," Charlotte stated with renewed passion, "but I intend that it will."

Bessie looked through the fabrics in her cupboard and found a piece that would fit the girl's needs.

"Can you have it ready for me today?" she asked.

"Yes. I'll have it today," the woman said.

"I'm grateful, Bessie," Charlotte said softly. "Forgive me. I should have asked before I blamed you for this."

The woman nodded in silence, but didn't take her eyes from her work.

Charlotte stood for a moment then asked, "Have you been in service long?"

"Yes, ma'm. Eight years."

"Where does Mr. Tellison go in the daytime?"

"He's a shipper."

"And what about the former housekeeper? What duties did she perform? Do you know?"

"Well, I can't really say." She fitted the material to the girl's neck. "There have been so many that have come and gone."

"So many?" Charlotte asked weakly. She looked quickly down at the woman's gray head, then turned her face upward again. Why? she wondered. Why would this be? Was it Mrs. Tellison's sharp tongue? Yes, it must be that. And she felt a wave of fresh apprehension take rise. She had to do well. She simply *had* to. Whatever the problems were with the others, they must not happen to her. Surely the Lord would help her, for He knew how completely dependent she was on Him to keep her from failing.

The duties at Lynnhampton were regimented but not unpleasant for Charlotte, and after a week, she gained the confidence of the underservants and her superiors, as well. But she relied wholly on continued prayer for help. Mr. Shannon felt less need to supervise, and spent more time in the estate offices than before.

Charlotte's search of the library uncovered a large collection of books and a Bible. She was overjoyed. On evenings when her work was finished, she was able to slip in, unnoticed, with her candle, to study and copy verses from the huge book.

Charlotte spent much time committing these scriptures to memory—to hide the word in her heart—and keep her mind from forbidden thoughts of Mr. Tellison.

Since the encounter in the hallway, she found that her thoughts reverted quite frequently to the tall, handsome man and she knew, also, that it was *very* wrong to permit herself one secret thought about a married man. Common sense warned her of that. It was foolhardy and sinful to entertain any fantasies of him in her heart. Charlotte was aware, though, that the feelings were not wholly on her side, for she found the man glancing at her rather frequently whenever he was in sight of her. She must not allow her testimony to be tarnished; she must not allow Satan to trick her into acting against her convictions. She must always be on guard against him.

After one of the servants accidentally knocked over a delicate porcelain vase, Charlotte took it upon herself to dust the china in the state dining room and hoped that she, herself, would not be so clumsy. It was while she was working in that room the following day, that she was summoned to her employer's apartment.

She made her way up the staircase and knocked. When Mr. Tellison told her to enter, she opened the door quietly and walked toward him.

"Miss Grey, when I give commands in this household, I expect them to be obeyed."

"Sir?" She couldn't imagine what he was talking about, and her heart beat with renewed apprehension. She gazed directly into his eyes for the answer.

"Bessie makes dresses just the way I want them, so will you please remove that ridiculous looking thing from your shoulders when you're around me? I'm not interested, in the least, in looking at a housekeeper who gives the appearance of one in mourning."

"No sir," she said quietly. "I will not." She wondered how on earth a blue flowered dress could possibly give the appearance of mourning, but she kept her thoughts to herself.

The young man was stunned and looked at the girl before him in unbelief. "You're going to disobey me, Miss Grey?"

She stood silently before him, refusing to lower her face or answer his challenge.

"Then, Miss Grey, I will remove it for you," he stated calmly.

Charlotte stubbornly maintained her unwillingness

to give in to his unreasonable demands, and noticed that he hesitated slightly before moving toward her. She refused to wince as he approached and stood directly in front of her. Then in one sweeping movement of his hand, he lifted the covering from her shoulders. He silently laid it across her clasped hands when she refused to take it from him.

He turned and walked to the fireplace with his hands behind him. As the man glanced back, he smiled at the determined set of her jaw and the lowered eyes that refused to follow him. Was the glistening that he detected in those beautiful blue eyes tears or anger?

"Sit down, please," he said at last. When she seated herself as commanded, he asked, "Do you have training in the arts?"

"Yes, sir."

"Then you read well?"

"Yes, sir."

"And play?"

She nodded affirmatively that she did.

"On what?"

"The pianoforte and harp." This was answered stiffly, while Charlotte sat poised and unbending in her chair.

He lifted his chin, raised his dark brows, and turned slightly at an angle. "Why did you leave your father's house?"

"He and my family died when our house burned to the ground." As Charlotte said it, the scene again came before her, and even though she tried hard to suppress the tears that gathered and glistened brightly in her eyes, she had to bite her lip to control the reaction. But it was futile; the tears rolled down unbidden.

Mr. Tellison gazed at her for a moment and said softly, "I am sorry Charlotte."

She lowered her head slightly to choke back a further display of emotion before it came to the surface.

"Do you have relatives?"

"No, sir. None that will admit it."

"I see." Then he seated himself at his table once more. "That will be all," he stated evenly, and resumed his work.

Charlotte rose and left the room, but she was aware that his dark eyes followed her until she closed the door behind her. As soon as she stood on the passage side, she hastily replaced the gauze about her shoulders. At that moment she saw, some thirty feet away, Madam Tellison approaching from the direction of her apartment. The woman's face was composed, but Charlotte read a sinister hatred behind those black eyes—a look that caused the girl to nod uneasily and say softly, "Madam," before she walked down the passage, in the opposite direction, with her head held high.

Charlotte felt thoroughly humiliated by the scene, and despised the shame of how her actions must have appeared to her mistress. Not once did she look back until she reached the bottom of the staircase. But the next thing she heard was a door closing loudly in the passage above. Charlotte was sure there were words between Mr. Tellison and his wife.

Later in the day, Bessie, under orders from Mr. Tellison, replaced a few inches of fabric to the neck of each gown.

The following day, Charlotte kept herself as busy as possible and was relieved that Mr. Tellison left the house early in the morning. Madam Tellison said nothing to her about the embarrassing situation the day before, so Charlotte tried to dismiss the incident from her mind as if it had never happened.

Cleaning the fine porcelains and dinnerware in the state dining room was one of the duties to which Charlotte committed herself with great pleasure. She had a special love for fine porcelains, though she no longer owned any.

The dish she held in her hand was a creation of a Mr. Bottger of Germany. She held it to the light to examine its fine workmanship; the excellent standard of quality bore his name. Then wiping it clean with her towel, she replaced it with extreme care, in the exact location from which it was taken. The pattern and name on the bottom of each piece was, by now, something that she could recite from memory, but she continued to go through the weekly process of looking at each one again simply for the pleasure it brought her. This day was no different from the previous ones and she used her towel on the pieces and continued her cleaning about the room. She held each piece with a firm grip lest she drop one.

"You like the porcelain, Miss Grey?"

Charlotte was so engrossed in her duties that she jumped at an unexpected voice behind her, and turned to find Madam Tellison standing in the doorway. "Yes, Madam, your collection is very fine."

"I'm pleased to see that you handle it with such great care for it's costly and quite ancient." Then as quickly as she had appeared, the woman left through the passage entrance and disappeared.

It was the first pleasant thing the woman had said to Charlotte since she came. Perhaps Mrs. Tellison was beginning to like her a little after all, she thought, and was changing her mind about getting rid of her. She felt a little better after that encounter, and found that her day began to go by a little more pleasantly.

Mr. Tellison returned from his shipping office shortly after supper and passed Charlotte in the hallway as she was returning from inspecting the first floor rooms.

"Charlotte, you told me that you played the harp." He unbuttoned his coat and turned toward the girl as he spoke.

"Yes, sir."

Then come to the music room," he said, "and play for me—in half an hour."

Charlotte nodded and hurried on to her apartment to tidy herself for she had had a busy day and was a little weary. She brushed, arranged her hair and gown to satisfaction, and studied her appearance in the mirror. For a fleeting moment, she was tempted to change into the dress that seemed to most enhance the blue of her eyes, but she quickly reprimanded herself for the foolishness of even allowing such a thought to enter her head.

At the appointed time, Charlotte knocked at the music room door. The man was sitting in a chair by the fire. He looked up and smiled, then nodded slightly when she came near and seated herself at the instrument. She tried to keep her eyes on the strings, but it took every ounce of willpower within her to do it, for he was stunningly handsome in his green velvet waistcoat and breeches. His dark eyes sparkled brilliantly. Charlotte was glad she was seated, for she was certain that her knees would have given way as mush if she were not.

She noticed that he sighed deeply then leaned back to listen.

It had been some weeks since Charlotte sat at a harp. She was a little tense knowing her employer's eyes were on her, studying her. After running her fingers lightly over the strings for a few moments, she regained the feeling for the instrument and was able to play with ease and enjoyment.

Mr. Tellison watched her under lids that only pretended to be closed. He studied her from head to toe while she played without being observed. Then, after half an hour, he told her that the recital was sufficient and added, "I will see, at a later time, if you read as well as you play."

Charlotte immediately put the instrument down and was preparing to leave the room when Mr. Tellison said, "Stay a while longer, Charlotte. Don't leave me. I'm having difficulty relaxing and I need someone to talk to. Come," he motioned to the seat beside him. "Sit down awhile and talk to me before you rush off." He slouched down a little, crossed his ankles, and leaned his head back to watch her while she sat in the chair next to him.

The fire was warm and crackling. Charlotte folded her hands in her lap as she sat in the warmth, but she was aware that her fingers formed a tight little ball. Sitting so near the man was unnerving. She refused to let her eyes wander to his face for she was sure he was watching her.

"You have beautiful hair, Charlotte."

"Thank you, sir." Her teeth moved over her lower lip to calm the tremors beginning to race down her body. Why was he taunting her like this?

"Are you happy here, Charlotte?"

"Yes, sir. Very." When she said this, she noticed that Mr. Tellison rose and stood with his back to the fire. She wished desperately that he would just tell her to leave so she could get back to the safety of her apartment. She liked being here with this man entirely too much; more than she wanted to admit. As it was, his face haunted her continuously during the day while she worked. Being here alone with him wasn't helping matters in the least.

"Have you ever considered marrying, Charlotte?"

"No, sir."

"Then you have never been in love?"

Charlotte didn't like the way the conversation was going. She rose quickly and said, "I must leave, sir, it's getting late."

"Charlotte," he said, "come here."

She stood perfectly still while her pulse hammered in her ears. To do what he asked was out of the question and she refused to move one inch toward the man or face him. Her eyes closed when she heard him repeat the command. Then turning, she looked at Mr. Tellison and said softly but firmly, "As a married man, sir, you have no right to talk to me like this."

"As a *what*?" He gave her a stunned little laugh and moved toward her.

"Your wife, sir. She trusts me and—"

"The woman isn't my wife," he laughed. "She's my *mother*!" He placed his warm hands on her shoulders and grinned in amusement. "No one *told* you she wasn't my wife? Surely the servants—or Shannon—" Then he stopped and stared into the blue eyes studying him. "Oh, Charlotte," he said wrapping his arms about her. "What am I to do with you?"

She closed her eyes and let herself be drawn close to his heart. The words were still trying to penetrate her fuzzy mind with the realization that he was not married at all—that she had just imagined it. Charlotte had not been held to a man's heart like this ever before, and it was delightfully pleasant. She was sure that her legs would give way if he should let go of her. But then she recalled the looks that Mrs. Tellison gave her, and she was certain that the woman would not approve of her behavior right now. Charlotte pulled away instantly.

"I really must leave, sir."

"But why? Don't you enjoy being with me, Charlotte?" he asked softly.

"Your mother would not—"

"My mother, Charlotte, would not like *anyone* who might take her son from her," he said tartly.

"Then that's why she—"

"Yes, that's why. But don't concern yourself."

"Oh, but I must, sir! As a Christian, I can't have her thinking badly of me. I *can't* ."

Mr. Tellison looked at Charlotte and the smile disappeared from his face. He walked back toward the fire. "I thought I was a Christian at one time," he whispered, "but I've been so busy and had so much on my mind—unsettling things."

"He loves you, you know," Charlotte said. "He will forgive if you ask Him to."

Mr. Tellison sighed and rubbed the back of his neck while his eyes closed and his face lifted. "I've wandered too far away, Charlotte."

"You need only say from deep within your heart, 'Lord, forgive me.' He is a just God, sir. He is forgiving."

"So, you heard John Wesley, too."

"Yes, sir. It was through his preaching that I first came to accept Christ as my Savior. He spoke at the village green in Withanham one morning and it was there that I first believed, and my family as well."

"I was happy in my belief once, but now . . ." He sighed and then glanced at the pretty girl standing beside him, facing him. "One day I'll ask Him to forgive me, but not yet. I can't do it now; my work wouldn't permit it for it's not . . ."

"Please, sir," Charlotte pleaded softly, earnestly. "Don't put it off. He is waiting to hear the words from your lips. You will not be truly happy until you do, you know."

"You just don't understand," he said rather harshly, "or you wouldn't say that. So much has crowded in, and I can't until . . ." Then he placed his hands gently on her shoulders and looked deeply into her eyes, eyes that held the brilliance of the firelight, and he let a finger trace along the line of her jaw before pressing it against her lips. "You're very persuasive, Charlotte Grey," he whispered softly, "and very beautiful. But don't concern yourself about my position with God. It's not your affair.''

The look in Mr. Tellison's eyes sent little tremors the full length of her body. When she looked into his eyes, she saw something burning that both thrilled and frightened her. *What is he doing to me?* she wondered uneasily.

The distance from Tellison Hall to the seaport town of Lynnhampton was approximately two miles, so Charlotte decided to make the trip since it was a pleasant one. She set about her tasks with a light heart and thought about the town's shops. Charlotte inspected the furniture in the music room, the salon, and then the state dining room. She picked up a porcelain bowl with flowers shaped into delicate garden roses and held it to the light to study its translucence against the bright light of the window overhead.

''The roses are magnificent on that piece, wouldn't you agree, Miss Grey?'' Mrs. Tellison asked quietly.

Charlotte saw Mrs. Tellison standing at the doorway gazing at her through those piercing black eyes.

''Yes, madam. I have never seen anything prettier.''

Mrs. Tellison walked slowly into the room with her stout face held high. She smiled slightly and continued to saunter about the room, inspecting first one piece and then another, pausing slightly before the rose decked bowl to adjust what she felt was some error in Charlotte's replacement of the piece. Then the woman passed on in her same rigid manner until she disappeared silently down the passage.

Charlotte thought it was strange behavior but then she dismissed it, for it had happened before. Today she felt too lighthearted at the thought of her morning excursion to let it bother her.

The road that Charlotte followed from Tellison Hall to the seaport town of Lynnhampton wound its way past the octagonal market place to the wharves beyond. Since she was in no particular hurry, Charlotte decided to follow the highway and see where it led. The thoroughfare became broader with handsome close-set row houses along both sides. From here the road followed along the bay. She saw a building with a brick facade and rows of symmetrical windows spaced pleasantly about a stone portico. A sign, in large letters above read, "Tellison Shipping." The name caught her entirely by surprise. "This," Charlotte said under her breath, "must be the master's business." And not wanting to be seen as if she were spying, she made a hasty exit down the street, and looked toward the water.

Charlotte's mind wandered back to Mr. Tellison. She found it increasingly difficult to keep his face and eyes from creeping into her thoughts. A man's attentions were something new to her. And pleasant. It quickened her heart and put a little spring in her step. But she reminded herself that his heart was not right before God. He admitted that it was not. She wondered what he was doing that stood as a barrier between him and his Lord—a thing that he felt was so great that he could not commit it to God.

The cold salt air smelled of fish. Seagulls squawked overhead. The dark vessels, anchored at the wharves, looked sullen and monstrous as they moved gently on the restless rise and fall of the waves.

She followed the wharf until she came to an intersecting of roadways. The one on her left circled back to the shops and market place and the one ahead plunged into an area of dingy, unkempt buildings. Her eyes focused on another shipping warehouse beside a miserable, decaying structure so dismal that she reasoned it must be a jail. Charlotte shuddered and hastily retraced her steps.

It was a special treat for her to slip into the chandler's and breathe in the deep scents. While she occupied herself with the pleasure, she happened to catch a glimpse of a black and gold carriage on the far side of the road. For a moment she stood motionless. "It's the Tellison carriage," she whispered. And while she watched from inside the shop, she saw Madam Tellison step from a doorway and enter the carriage with Samuel's help. Charlotte studied the sign above the opposite establishment. "T. A. Heinz, Lawyer," she whispered to herself. She wouldn't have given the incident a second thought except that the woman had an unusual expression on her droll face.

"Oh well," she said softly, "It is none of my affair." She turned her face westward in the direction of the Hall, and would have continued homeward had she not heard singing. From somewhere came the strains of a song—a song familiar to her ears and sung by two men's voices. It made her heart beat faster. A large gathering congregated on the green near the market place. It had been so long since she had had any real fellowship with believers. She turned and hurried back to the assembly and stood along the fringes to see who the men were. She immediately recognized the thin, clean-looking man with the good complexion. Yes, it was he; Mr. Wesley, himself.

He told of the love of God and the blood of Jesus that cleanses from all sin. He stated that only in Christ is there peace. They were wonderful words spoken with clarity and conviction. Charlotte's eyes filled with tears. She thought of past Sunday afternoons when she sat with her family in Chapel and heard those words of encouragement. They were uplifting and full of hope. Oh, how she missed them. Charlotte hung onto each word and drank it in as a man dying of thirst cries out for water. She thought about Mr.

Tellison and wondered why he felt that he couldn't come to so merciful a God and place his heavy, disagreeable burden before Him. Why did he want to carry it around with him when he could be rid of it so easily? Charlotte sighed. Then her thoughts came back forcefully to Mr. Wesley's words.

Charlotte was one of the last to leave. Would she ever hear such words spoken again? Would the men be there the following week? It would give her something to look forward to; to hope for. The words rang in her ears, thrilling her heart all the way back to the manor house.

CHAPTER 3

CHARLOTTE AWOKE TO A December morning, a frosty morning that caused a thin layer of ice in the water pitcher. The panes in the windows bore delicate feathery designs of icy lacework from the top to the bottom. The sun was hidden beneath vast layers of angry, racing clouds that periodically dropped snowflakes that settled on bare, black branches.

Mr. Shannon came into the morning room to go over the accounts. From where she sat, Charlotte could see the steam pouring from the windows in the wash house. She was thankful that she was snug inside the House and was grateful that she had somewhere to live and a job in which she felt reasonably secure.

The Lord is good, she thought, *so good to me.*

By evening Charlotte prepared to retire early. She bathed and was brushing the long curls about her shoulders, when she received a summons to the drawing room. These summons were growing more frequent and Charlotte was a little apprehensive. Mr.

Tellison would place his hand on her arm or look at her with eyes that made her tremble. He was very handsome and attentive. It took all the determination in her heart not to react to his charms when she was alone with him. She must not lose sight of the fact that he was not living a life pleasing to God. And until he was. . . . But even that was foolish for her to consider, for she could never be anything more to him than a servant; she was penniless.

Charlotte threw the shawl over her shoulders and allowed her hair to fall loosely over her back. She would not admit how much she enjoyed being with her employer, talking with him.

Mr. Tellison was facing the window and gazing out over the bare moonswept elms beyond his courtyard gates when she entered.

"Be seated, Charlotte," he said quietly. She placed her candle on the small table near his chair and then sat down as directed.

Mr. Tellison paced the floor with his hands thrust into the pockets of his robe and without looking at her he said, "Charlotte, read to me for I can't sleep."

She took the book he offered and read for some time while the man continued to walk back and forth across the floor. When he sat down next to her, Charlotte had to force herself to keep her eyes on the pages.

Mr. Tellison was slightly amused with her plight.

Finally, in desperation, she lowered the book and said, "Do you wish me to continue, sir?"

"Of course. Why wouldn't I? I'm enjoying myself and I am beginning to relax."

She commenced again but he interrupted her by saying, "Charlotte, you are very beautiful. Has anyone ever told you that?" he asked gazing steadily at her.

Charlotte nodded but she prayed for stern control of her voice.

After a few moments, Mr. Tellison said "That will be enough reading for now." Charlotte replaced the book and rose to take her candle that was now burning low.

"Don't leave yet," he said. "Tell me, Charlotte, what do you spend your time reading and copying in the library?"

"Scripture verses, sir."

"Nothing else?"

"No, sir."

"I heard Wesley the last time he was in Lynnhampton but he made me very uncomfortable."

"It's a matter of asking God for forgiveness, sir, and you will find that your uncomfortable feelings will turn into feelings of peace."

"You make it sound so simple," he stated flatly.

"It is, sir."

"No, Charlotte. In my case it's not that simple," he returned harshly.

By now Charlotte's candle was so low that the wick no longer burned. She knelt by the fire to light what was left of it, but Mr. Tellison interrupted her. "Allow me," he said reaching for a fresh candle on the mantlepiece. When it burned brightly, he handed it to her.

Before she could pull her woolen shawl about her, he placed his hands on the girl's arms and gazed into her eyes. She tried to pull from his grasp but he held her too securely. "You please me very much, Charlotte," he whispered, "and I shall think carefully about what you have said."

But before she realized what he did, or could object to it, his lips lowered to hers. The kiss was gentle and his hands were warm on her arms. But she knew it was wrong for her to accept such liberties even though she enjoyed his nearness and liked the feel of his lips on hers. Without a word she pulled from his grasp, turned, and walked from the room.

Charlotte moved so rapidly that she failed to see the figure of Mrs. Tellison advancing silently in the shadows at the far end of the passage.

The warm, intimate touch of Mr. Tellison's hands on her arm continued with Charlotte the remainder of the evening. It was the first time that a man had touched her like that, or kissed her, and although she tried to dismiss it from her thoughts, she found that she couldn't do it. It awakened fresh, new sensations that told her she was no longer a girl. She was a woman capable of a woman's strong feelings. She wondered exactly what the master meant by, "You please me very much."

In the days following, Charlotte performed her duties mechanically while she assessed the situation. Mr. Tellison gave her pleasure. Of that there was no doubting. Although she had a spark of desire within her to return to him, she still possessed a fear that she must be on guard at all times. Mr. Tellison was unsettling. And handsome. His chestnut hair was luxuriously thick and his dark eyes were bright, shining with a light all their own.

"But it won't do," she flatly reminded herself. "It won't do at all."

Mr. Tellison spent much time away from the Hall in the days that followed. Snatches of conversation suggested to Charlotte that the master had problems with a rival shipper but she could not make out where or how. It was none of her business, of course. When he spent evenings at the manor he called her to read or play for him, or just sit with him. At times he would pace endlessly, but she could always feel his eyes upon her while she remained with him.

A few weeks prior to Christmas, Charlotte received a summons to appear before Mr. Tellison early in the day.

"We'll prepare a supper one week before Christmas for the entertaining of the captains and officers of my ships." Mr. Tellison leaned back in his chair and looked directly at his housekeeper, not taking his eyes from her face while he spoke. "There will be forty men altogether. Since the evening will include business, I want you there the whole time to entertain my guests on the harp. I'm having an emerald gown made especially for you for the evening." For a few moments the man continued to study the girl before him. "Mrs. Tellison has engaged a hair dresser for the occasion," he added, "and the fellow will arrange yours as well."

"Thank you, sir."

"Talk to the cook about a menu."

Charlotte nodded and waited to be excused but when he continued to study her, in an absent-minded manner and said nothing, she took the initiative into her own hands and left.

The two days preceding the event were filled with marvelous odors from the cook's kitchen in the form of puddings, breads, fruit tarts, and Marchpane. The woman gave a mad flurry of orders to the underservants for baskets of apples, raisins, plums, nuts, flour, spices, and candied peel to be brought to the kitchen and prepared for her use.

The household teemed with excitement. Charlotte supervised but went out of her way to ask Mrs. Tellison's unneeded advice after the woman walked about with her dark eyes blazing, demanding to know why she wasn't consulted on the menus. Since Charlotte could not explain why, she dreamed up ways to use the woman's suggestions and bring her into the bustle of activity. She invited the woman to help her and advise the arranging of the state dining room— the silver, linens, and china. Although Mrs. Tellison's presence was more of a hindrance than a help, Charlotte never failed to thank her for her work.

On the morning of the banquet, Charlotte went to her apartment to have her hair arranged for the special occasion. The Frenchman worked marvels with his comb and brushes. He carefully coiffed her hair smooth in the center front, allowing the high sweep to end in luxurious curls that lay down the back of her neck. The man marveled at his handiwork.

"Eet ees lovelee, madam. You are a princess feet for a keeng." And he danced about in sheer delight at the beauty of the girl sitting serenely before him. "All you lack are jewels for that lovelee neck of yours. You weel be elegant, madam." Charlotte didn't argue but she smiled at the thought of a jewel on the neck of a servant!

The magnificent delicacies were in readiness and filled the kitchen table by five o'clock, awaiting their transfer to the state dining room in one hour.

In the center of the dining table, Charlotte placed an elaborate network of mistletoe and pine bows intermingled with scented, red candles which gave a truly festive air to the occasion. Charlotte inspected the lovely array and hoped Mr. Tellison and his mother would be pleased.

When Charlotte looked up, she saw Mr. Tellison looking at her from across the room. "Sir, I didn't hear you enter," she said softly.

"So I noticed." He walked to where she stood and put his warm hands on the girl's arms. "You look beautiful, Charlotte. Stunning," he whispered, looking into her eyes.

Her master's eyes moved slowly upward to study her wheat-colored hair. "Yes, he did it perfectly. Now hold still one moment." With this, Mr. Tellison reached into his pocket and held something in his hand for her to see. Charlotte drew in her breath and stared at a magnificent emerald bordered about with small diamonds. She was speechless. All she could do was stare first at the gem and then at the man who, by now, was smiling his droll one-sided smile that had become so familiar and precious to her.

"It's yours, Charlotte. A Tellison emerald."

"No. Oh, no, sir," cried Charlotte drawing back. "Please don't ask me to wear it."

"Oh, but I insist." And before she could move away from him, she felt herself being pulled closely to face him while he placed the emerald in the smooth area at the front of her hair. Immediately Mr. Tellison propelled her to a small mirror. He stood behind her while she gazed at the reflection and saw the afternoon sun catch the lights of both her pale hair and the emerald, against his own dark features. Then whirling about she looked imploringly into his eyes.

"But I cannot. What will Mrs. Telli—"

"Mrs. Tellison, Charlotte? Frankly, I don't care!" he said harshly. And he turned abruptly about to depart from the room, leaving behind him an unhappy girl who dreaded the appearance of the older woman in a matter of minutes.

When the clock chimed six, Mr. Tellison promptly appeared and accompanied his guests into the room where Charlotte remained as well hidden as she dared before the inevitable encounter. From her spot in the corner she silently directed the placing of dishes on the sideboard while the men filed to their seats amidst a general buzz of light-hearted chatter.

Mrs. Tellison was totally unaware of Charlotte's presence in the room. She was seated at the end of the table opposite her son and apparently basking in the ridiculous flattery of the men about her.

While the joints of beef and venison were being served, the eyes of one of the captains caught the light of the girl's hair as she moved about the sideboard. "Where did you find the charming girl at your sideboard, Mr. Tellison?" he asked. Immediately all the gazes about him turned in Charlotte's direction. "Is she a servant? No, a relative, surely. But come, sir, tell us who she is!"

"My housekeeper, gentlemen." He merely grinned and said no more.

"Aha! Lucky man." By now the infection spread and all eyes focused fully on the girl. She was so busy serving that she was only vaguely aware of the remarks and glances until Mrs. Tellison turned and discovered Charlotte with the diamond-emerald sparkling in her hair. The black anger in the woman's eyes, and the lustful glances of the men about the table, caused the girl to blush.

"Come now," the master called, "Surely you have seen beautiful girls in every port from here to Calcutta. Resume your feasting." And with this he put a large chunk of venison into his mouth to encourage the conversation to resume its normal but somewhat embellished hum.

Hearty appetites made deep dents into the quantities of meats and fish, soups, carrots, cheeses and tarts. When the final course was set before the men, they marveled at the elaborately molded Marchpane in forms of ships in full rigging with almonds and pistachios carefully placed as cannons and decorative bows.

After the table was cleared, Charlotte settled back in a chair by the window nearest the corner and took up her needlework for occupation during the ensuing business.

"Gentlemen," the master announced. "Good King George has seen fit to renew our contracts for the coming year."

"Huza!" echoed the men.

"We continue with excellent records and few deaths. This I attribute to installing the ventilators, captains." And each man, in turn, agreed with his employer. "Well then, it was worth the expense, for the health of our cargo is money to shipping," said Mr. Tellison. "Our consignments of tobacco arrive in excellent condition and our customers remain with us."

"Thanks to the merchants, sir, who keep the planters in debt with low payments for tobacco. The planters are a special breed; wasteful, spendthrifts, the lot of 'em. They order a great amount of finery, in return for the hogsheads of tobacco they sell, so they can live like gentlemen. They've no right."

"But gentlemen," Mr. Tellison warned, "Let's not forget that unrest in America is growing. The colonists are unhappy with the duties the king imposes. If war should ensue . . ."

"It's not likely, sir. The colonists are an ignorant backwoods lot—totally disorganized. They would not have a chance against our strong navy."

"I'm not so sure, gentlemen," said the master. "Not as long as France remains our enemy. But as long as we have cargo, we earn money. And this year looks good. After that, well—we shall see. There is Australia to be considered."

"Aye, sir. Aye, that it is."

"Now," the master continued, "I want to thank you, my captains, for helping the company to be the greatest in all England." And with that the former hum of conversation resumed with the men talking among themselves.

Charlotte wondered at the things that were said, but since she understood none of it, she quietly continued her sewing until the master announced that Miss Grey would favor them with a few selections on the harp.

Charlotte dreaded being the focus of attention for such a group. The greedy looks on their faces spelled out the lust in their hearts. As long as she played, the men gave her their undivided attention. Charlotte's slender fingers plucked the strings while her hair and jewel caught the lights from the candles nearby and glistened brilliantly. The master smiled and cared not in the least that his mother glared hateful revenge on her son for this night's deeds.

When the final number ended, Mr. Tellison nodded his full approval before excusing his housekeeper. He then accompanied his men toward the billiard and game room to amuse themselves at billiards or whist.

Charlotte wondered what Mrs. Tellison said to her son. But when she, herself, was summoned to the drawing room late that night, Charlotte returned the jewel to him in spite of his stern objections otherwise.

"I am happy, sir, that your shipping is profitable," she said softly. "What is it that you ship?"

"Cargo," he said harshly.

She immediately regretted that she asked for it was no concern of hers, and he let her know it in no uncertain terms. Then she sighed.

"I'm sorry, Charlotte. We send cargo over and bring back tobacco from the Virginia plantations. The tobacco is then picked up, at our English warehouses, by our merchants." But still he would not tell what he shipped to the colonies; nor would she ask—ever again.

When Charlotte climbed into bed she felt a slight chilling come over her. It could best be likened to the feeling she experienced when, at the preacher's fireplace months before, she clasped her cloak about her to try to dispel the foreboding that overtook her before she left Withanham for the last time. With the passing weeks, Charlotte wrestled with her emotions. She yearned—as a hungry man yearns for bread—for the touch of Mr. Tellison's hand or the gentle look of his eyes upon her. She longed for the meetings, but she was determined to keep her distance. It was a battle to keep her mind on her work. She asked God to intervene for she found that her ears were attuned constantly, during the day, to the chiming of the long clock in the passage heralding the evening hours and the summons to read to him or play the harp. She would not admit that she was in love, hopelessly in love, with her employer.

Mr. Tellison called for Charlotte late one evening after she had already retired for the night. She dressed hurriedly, ran a brush through her hair, and went to him.

When Charlotte entered the library, she left the door open. He had learned that to insist otherwise was futile—draft or no draft.

The young man paced without speaking a word. She waited quietly by the fire until he was ready to speak. The sight of him, even at this distance, caused her to tremble slightly, for the love she had for him was growing in spite of her desire otherwise.

He continued to pace. "Have you ever had a lover, Charlotte?"

"No, sir."

"None whatsoever?" he asked.

She shook her head negatively.

Then he looked at the pretty girl standing before him. The familiar smile appeared on his face. After a few moments he walked toward her, put his hands on her shoulders and gently but firmly attempted to pull her to him. Charlotte struggled to free herself. Her hand reached for the candle and she turned quickly toward the door.

"Charlotte," he called.

She stood where she was with her back to the master, saying nothing.

"Do you find me that disagreeable, Charlotte?" he asked softly.

Without turning, she leaned her head forward and shook it gently while the curls glistened and moved about her small shoulders. "No, sir."

"Then come back," he said quietly.

She turned her face slowly toward the young man, fighting the desire to run back to his arms for she was well aware of the pleasure his nearness gave her. "Please don't do this to me," she whispered.

Mr. Tellison moved forward and placed his warm hands on her upper arms. For a few moments he let his face brush against her hair, and then her cheek, and neck.

Suddenly Charlotte pulled from the young man's arms and for one moment of time raised her misty eyes to his before moving toward the doorway. When she closed the door softly behind her, Charlotte leaned heavily against the wall for support while a tear slipped down her cheek. From somewhere she received the strength against an overwhelming force.

Mrs. Tellison called for Charlotte early on a Wednesday morning and when the girl entered the woman's apartment, she found the curtains drawn and her mistress lying in her bed.

"Madam," Charlotte asked with alarm evident in her voice, "are you ill? Can I do something for you—get you something?"

"It's the headache. I am troubled by it at times."

"I'm so sorry," Charlotte answered with true concern.

As the woman spoke, she did not look at Charlotte, but kept her face to the ceiling and placed her thick arm across her forehead. "There is a matter, Miss Grey, that I want you to take care of if you go into town today."

"Of course. I'll be glad to do anything I can."

"Miss Grey, look on my dressing table. You will find an article wrapped in a paper." The woman continued with her eyes closed and in apparent pain.

Charlotte jumped quickly to her feet and walked to the table for the parcel. "Yes, Madam."

"Open it and look inside."

The girl obediently unwrapped the thing and found that it contained a small porcelain dish of a very delicate Chinese motif. Charlotte remembered the dish for she didn't especially care for it. "Yes, Madam, I have it."

The woman continued to speak with her eyes closed. "There is a small shop in Lynnhampton that deals in old porcelains. Hargrove's, it is."

"Yes, I know where it is."

"He buys old pieces for his business and I want him to have it. Take care not to tell him that it is mine for I don't want him bothering me for more pieces."

"Yes, Madam."

"Wrap it well and put it in a cloth so you won't drop it."

Again the girl did as she was told and rewrapped the bowl with care.

The woman's arms were still over her face when Charlotte announced. "It is rewrapped, Madam, and I will take good care of it."

"Very well."

Charlotte started to leave but before she latched the door behind her, Mrs. Tellison called her name.

"Miss Grey, Mr. Tellison is fond of the thing even though he forgets it is in the cupboard. Please don't mention it to him."

"Yes, Madam. I hope you will be feeling better. Can I have the cook bring something to you before I leave?"

"No, Miss Grey," she said with rising irritation seeping into her voice.

How curious, thought Charlotte, *that Madam would want to sell a porcelain dish that is a particular favorite of the master. It isn't reasonable to think that she would do it for the price it would bring for surely she doesn't need the money for her pockets. Perhaps it would be for spite, for there seems so little harmony between them.* But coming to no reasonable conclusion about it, she hurried out the door with her parcel in hand.

Mr. Hargrove's pottery shop was a strangely constructed two storied edifice. It was on a likewise strangely shaped parcel of ground that was wider in the rear than in the front. The whole of the outside was a rough plaster and on three sides, huge paned windows displayed a varied collection of wares.

Charlotte went into the shop and waited. When she pushed the package toward the man, Mr. Hargrove nodded, took the porcelain, and examined it carefully. On one occasion during the inspection, he glanced up at the young woman before him with a slightly quizzical glint in his watery eyes. "It is a very old piece and quite valuable." Then he laid the dish down, pursed his lips and tapped one long thin finger on the table to help him think. "I think ten pounds a fair sum." And he took the money from his drawer. "It has had excellent care. Not a crack or a scratch on it."

"Yes, sir." The girl nodded and smiled slightly.

He handed her the cash and asked, "Your name is what, Miss?"

"Charlotte, sir. Charlotte Grey."

The man watched her closely with his blue eyes.

She took the money, put it into her pocket, and left the shop, content that the transaction went as Mrs. Tellison wanted it to.

Because of the large sum of money on her person, Charlotte cut her browsing short. Since the preachers were not on the green, she walked back toward the House.

Mrs. Tellison was as Charlotte left her earlier—in her bed and still. But she had shifted herself so that she faced the wall away from the doorway.

"I have ten pounds, madam," the girl whispered. "It is the price of the dish. Shall I put the money on your writing table?"

"Please put it in the painted box on the right side of my writing table, Miss Grey."

It was a few moments before Charlotte located the specified box, but she found it and placed the ten pounds inside as directed. "Will there be anything else, madam?" she asked softly.

"No. That's all."

The evening was cold so Charlotte sat before her fire to hem sheets. She remained fully clothed due to Mr. Tellison's frequent calls and she didn't want to be caught in an awkward situation.

At eight o'clock the bell summoned her to Mr. Tellison's apartment. She took her candle and proceeded up the tower staircase to his door.

"Close the door behind you," he said firmly.

She was determined that he would not trick her with soft words into doing something she felt was wrong. "No, sir," she answered.

"Then the responsibility for my health is on your head."

She glanced into his eyes. "Yes, sir, it is." Her answer was straightforward and without wavering.

"You promised, you know, to finish the book for me," he said pointing to the chair. Instead of the usual pacing, Mr. Tellison sat across from Charlotte and settled back in his chair to observe the girl while she read. His face had the droll smile that she had become accustomed to, but tonight she detected a sparkle about his eyes—a brilliance that was intense and unnerving.

For some time he did not interrupt. When, at last, he rose and sauntered about the room, he pushed the door closed slightly without her knowledge of it. He continued his pacing and moved back to the fireplace before seating himself again.

She continued reading for several pages more until Mr. Tellison interrupted and said, "That will be all. Please bring me the book."

Charlotte hesitated but walked to where he sat and handed the volume to him. It was at that moment he took hold of her hand and held it firmly in his. Charlotte tried to pull away but to no avail.

"Please sir, you are hurting me," she cried softly. Instead of lessening his grasp of her, he held more firmly and reached up with his other hand to grasp her free arm. Charlotte's heart beat intensely within her breast. His gaze was like nothing she had seen before. In her forced, seated position he whispered, "Charlotte, I love you." He spoke soothingly and tenderly to the distraught girl until she relaxed somewhat. His eyes did not leave the searching of her face and when she was quiet he spoke softly once more. "Charlotte, I love you," he repeated. With this, he pulled her down to him and kissed her tenderly at first, and then with passion. And in spite of herself, she responded until he released her slightly to speak.

"Charlotte," he said tenderly, putting his hand to her face and moving her lower jaw to one side as the manner of the master was, "I have a small house a few miles from here near the sea. A lovely out of the way spot; secluded and well wooded, it is. You may live in it, have servants and have a carriage of your own if you will permit me, shall we say, certain pleasures and . . ."

"No! No, Mr. Tellison, no!" she cried trying to release both her arms which he now held in his own to cease her struggles. She turned her face from his and closed her eyes while the hot tears of humiliation squeezed out beneath her long lashes. Then his eyes sparkled. He smiled and pulled her down once more while she struggled to escape. His embrace was long and tender. His lips were like fire on her own, and she felt weak and trembling, a helpless prisoner.

"Oh, Charlotte, my dearest Charlotte," he whispered softly, releasing her slightly. It was then that she tore loose from his hold and headed for the door.

The passage was pitch black without her candle but she groped her way to the staircase. Somehow she managed to make her way back to her room in total darkness and fling herself onto her bed to weep bitter tears.

Charlotte slept but when she awoke at some undetermined hour, the pale moonlight was sifting in through the diamond panes of glass gently bathing her room with its gossamer softness. She pulled a blanket over her to relieve the unearthly chill that crept stealthily over her whole being. The light from the window disappeared as suddenly as it had come and her room was plunged into a thick darkness. Outside, the wind moaned amidst the elms and towers, but she shut it out by slipping into a fitful slumber with bits and pieces of her life floating past her unseeing eyes.

Little did she realize that the mad, frenzied days to follow would do nothing to lift her from the depths that overtook her for the second time in her life.

CHAPTER 4

A SHEET OF RAIN WAS SMASHING against her window when Charlotte rose from her bed and spied a paper shoved under the door of her room. She bent to retrieve it and opened the letter with trembling fingers. The scrawled hand read,

Dearest Charlotte,

You answered my question as I was hoping you would. I wanted to be sure you wouldn't be bought with money. When I return I shall ask you one more question, my love.

God has shown me His mercy and forgiveness. Now I go to make my life right.

Ben Tellison

Charlotte folded the precious paper and slipped it into her bosom while she bent to stir the fire until it blazed hot for her bath. *He's made his life right. Oh, thank you, Lord.* Her prayers had been answered. She whispered to herself, "What will he ask me? Can it be that he truly loves me, that he wishes to marry me?"

53

The memory of his kiss, the nearness of him, the blazing look in his eyes, came back in full force and beat against her brain with fiery pleasure. "And if it's not that—not marriage—would it be so wrong to love him? Am I not all alone in the world? Who would care, really? Could I leave him forever and not feel the ache of parting?" And a small voice, an eager voice, seemed to say, "No, it would not be wrong. Take pleasure where you find it." But just as swiftly another small voice, a calm but strong voice whispered, "You could not do it and hold your head high. You could not—would not—for you belong to Me. I will give you strength to do what is right."

A tear squeezed out from beneath her lids and slid slowly down her cheek. She again remembered his words, "Charlotte, I love you."

She bathed and dressed carefully and due to her uneasiness, tucked her few remaining shillings into her bosom before she flung her shawl about her shoulders to avoid chilling after her bath.

Charlotte proceeded with her duties of checking food supplies and menus, but in spite of her efforts to try to concentrate, she found herself coming back to the heavenly words written in that letter. Her heart was overjoyed that the man she loved had found forgiveness. God would make everything right; He would work out her problems in His own time. Of this, she had no doubts.

With a light heart, Charlotte set about the dusting of the porcelains and was nearly finished when a maid came in with a note. It stated that Mrs. Tellison had left earlier, for London, to visit a doctor and would not return for several days.

"So," she thought with relief, "I can be at ease for a few days, at least." And she continued her duties with a much lighter heart.

The rain no longer pummeled the windows but fell

in the kind of steady flow that soaks the ground and puts a touch of life to every growing thing. A strange silence fell about the Great House.

The passage clock was chiming nine when Charlotte became aware of wheels rumbling over the stones of the carriage path and approaching the rear entrance to the House. Within moments, the little maid returned and said, "Miss Grey, there is a gentleman waiting to see you in the small entrance passage."

"A gentleman?" Charlotte was stunned. "Did he give you his name?"

"No, Miss. He said he was from London and it was about urgent business."

Charlotte put the towel carefully aside and made her way down the passage. Her brain tried to fathom the meaning of the early caller; she was unknown to anyone outside the Hall.

The gentleman rose when she came into view. "Miss Grey, I am Mr. Heinz, a lawyer. Will you accompany me, please, for I need to speak with you." He motioned for the girl to come with him.

Charlotte was so stunned that she complied without resistance. The man steered her beyond the rain soaked carriage path to a walkway hidden by trees. For some moments she tried to recall where she had heard the man's name. It sounded vaguely familiar.

The rain had ceased except for a fine mist while Mr. Heinz began his probing. Charlotte turned to the man and studied him closely as she accompanied him.

"Miss Grey, were you in Lynnhampton this Wednesday past?"

"Yes, sir, I was."

"And did you, at that time, go into Mr. Hargrove's pottery?"

"Yes, sir." Charlotte put her hand to her throat to control the fervent pounding of the blood in her temples. She had *promised* not to mention Madam's name in connection with the dish. "I always go in to browse, sir."

"But did you browse?"

"No, sir, I did not. I had a matter of business to attend to." She drew her shawl about her as she began to chill.

"What was the nature of the business, Miss Grey?"

"Tell me, sir," she said, "just why you question me on this matter." She looked directly into his steel gray eyes.

The straightforward look of the girl disarmed the man. "Just answer my questions, Miss Grey," he said sternly.

"I sold a dish, sir."

"And was it your dish to sell?"

"Why do you ask?" she inquired with some irritation rising in her voice. "It was a matter of selling a dish and receiving payment for it."

"Then I shall have to ask you to come with me to Lynnhampton. Perhaps you will explain to the shopkeeper about the matter."

"But why? Surely it was an honest dealing."

"In that case you wouldn't object talking with him. I am a lawyer, Miss Grey, and I would advise you to be honest. Come. My carriage is waiting."

"But I can't just leave like this, sir, for I am an employee of this household and I must speak to Mr. Shannon about this matter before I leave."

The man took a firm hold on her arm and propelled Charlotte toward the waiting carriage. "Mr. Shannon, Miss Grey, already has been informed of the matter and wants it cleared as quickly as possible. Now if you please, allow me . . . " He helped the girl into the carriage, called to his groom, and they left with some speed down the elm avenue toward the town. The two rode in absolute silence with Charlotte staring in numbed unbelief at the man sitting on the seat

56

opposite her—a man who nervously set about studying papers that he removed from the case on the seat beside him.

Charlotte looked at her hands that were, by now, clenched in a tight, little knot. As she studied her fingers, the man beside her, also, did some studying on his own and he had painful misgivings about the assignment that he agreed to do for Mrs. Tellison.

Madam will explain all of this to the man, thought Charlotte, for when she realizes that it has put me to a great inconvenience as well as the questioning of my character, she will explain things and this ridiculous ordeal will have a quick end to it so I can return to the House.

The carriage rumbled through the main street of Lynnhampton past the shops and market place and onto the road that angled toward the wharf. From here they made another left turn and stopped in the squalid section that she remembered from her stroll.

When Charlotte was helped from the carriage she saw before her the huge, dingy, decayed structure that she had guessed was the jail, and realized that it was into this very place she was being taken. She could only stare in dumb silence.

"Come quickly," Mr. Heinz ordered. And she did. What else could she do? They climbed several worn, stone steps, entered a dreary passage, and followed into a room of sizable proportions.

Seated on a bench and with his back to them, was the shopkeeper, Mr. Hargrove.

The lawyer motioned for Charlotte to accompany him forward and to stand before a judge. "Miss Grey is being accused, sir, of taking a costly dish to the shop of Mr. Hargrove and selling it." He said this while he pointed to the shopkeeper seated to the left.

"Is this true, Mr. Hargrove?" asked the judge.

The thin man rose with great haste and said, "Yes, sir, this is the young woman."

"Proceed, Mr. Heinz," admonished the judge.

"It was wrapped in paper." Then he turned to Mr. Hargrove. "Show the paper, please," instructed Mr. Heinz.

Mr. Hargrove presented the paper that was around the bowl.

"Now, Mr. Hargrove, will you please tell us what happened at your shop," said the judge as the lawyer and Charlotte were seated.

The shopkeeper related the tale in accurate detail while the lawyer and judge listened. When he finished, Mr. Heinz said, "Thank you, Mr. Hargrove. You may leave."

Turning to Charlotte, the lawyer stated, "Madam Tellison told me that an expensive dish was missing from her house and she suspected you took it. She mentioned that you were found, on numerous occasions, handling her porcelains with great interest. She described the dish to me and asked me to investigate the matter for her. I went to Mr. Hargrove and the dish was there."

Charlotte was so completely dumb with shock that she sat as immovable as the bench on which she sat.

"I find it interesting that you refuse to discuss any knowledge of the transaction other than the fact that you sold it," conceded Mr. Heinz.

"I was told to sell the dish." Charlotte's voice rose in indignation and her lips formed a firm, thin line against the man's accusations.

"And you kept the money."

"No, sir. I took it directly to Mrs. Tellison as directed by her."

"Did you hand it to her?"

"No, sir. I put it in the designated box."

"Did she see you do it?"

"No, sir. She had her face to the wall."

"Then why didn't she find the money when she looked for it?"

"I cannot say."

"Could it be that you failed to put it there?" he accused loudly.

With this, Charlotte looked unwaiveringly into the cold eyes of the lawyer as she spoke. "Before Christ, as my witness and my Savior, I placed the money in the box by Mrs. Tellison's bed."

"Madam Tellison did not know that you sold the dish nor did she find the ten pounds in her drawer."

At this, Charlotte's eyes filled with tears and she felt she would stagger if a sudden warmth, a strength, an abiding Presence, had not intervened to buoy her up and give her the ability to endure the bitterly false accusations facing her. And, for some inexplicable reason, her lips were now sealed against further comment or explanation as to her actions.

"This is a serious crime, Miss Grey, and serious crimes beget serious consequences." By now both the judge and Mr. Heinz were mopping the perspiration from their brows. "You are sentenced, Miss Grey," the judge informed her, "as a felon. There are two routes of punishment for you. Hanging or transporting. The one automatically overrides the other. If you stay, you will hang, for no jury will acquit you on such dire charges. You will go as a convict to escape that hanging."

Charlotte rose and stood as a statue, void of feeling and numb. What alternatives did she have? None. The men did not believe her though she spoke the truth. She closed her eyes and realized that once again in the space of a short span, her life was torn asunder from any shred of reality and plunged into the depths of horror. She vividly recalled the stories of rotting corpses of criminal justice when nothing more than a handkerchief was involved.

A jailer was summoned to lead her beneath the ground level of the building to a darkened corner of a room and immediately he put a chain about her ankle. Numbly Charlotte looked about her as her eyes adjusted to the darkness. She studied the moldy stone of the wall, the timbered ceiling, and the cold damp floor littered with musty straw. Only one window gave light from the outside world.

Charlotte stood on the cold stones and wondered anxiously what to do. Surely she couldn't sit in such filth. She watched the jailer shuffle down the passage and return with a large bundle of clean straw that he tossed unceremoniously toward her. Then he handed her something tied in a huge checkered cloth.

She spread the clean straw, then opened the cloth. Inside she found her cloak, gowns, and papers with the scriptures carefully lettered on each page. The parcel gave her a slight lift to her fainting spirits. *Someone at the Hall knows of my plight and will surely tell Mr. Tellison. Without doubt he will come for me.*

Charlotte refolded her belongings and leaned back on the straw to try to unravel the horrible web of events that held her.

Why, she kept asking herself, *did madam do this to me? Does she realize the crime and consequences facing me?* Charlotte tried desperately to ply her reasoning powers into some form of a plan before the jailer returned—some method of communication to let the servants at the House know of her plight.

When the jailer came by with boiled bread and water, Charlotte cried out. "Please, sir, will you deliver a message for me? I was taken from Tellison Hall falsely, for I've done nothing wrong. Tell Mr. Shannon to come here. I will pay you to take the message. Oh, please . . . "

The jailer was irritated by her pleas but he liked the idea of payment. Licking his thin lips he whispered, "What will ye pay me, criminal?"

"A shilling, sir, a shilling. Now listen carefully," she cried in anguish. "Tell Mr. Shannon—or any of the servants—that I am here." And she reached into her bosom to produce the promised coin. "Please, sir, please don't fail me."

The man sneered, took the coin and left Charlotte clinging desperately to her only remaining hope. She watched the man disappear beyond her sight before she turned silently to the bread and water.

For the remainder of the day she hoped that someone from the House would miss her and search for her. But as the hours began to slip away and the little bit of light from the window turned to gray, illusions of rescue faded. A great terror seized her. She was a criminal. A branded criminal. The devastating blow pounded in her brain, shutting out all reason; shutting out all reality.

"Oh, God," she cried beseechingly, "deliver me from this horrible place and set my feet in respectable surroundings once again. Even if I have to scrub floors or scour pans." And the words of the circuit preacher came back to her: "You may not always understand His ways. . . . "

Charlotte turned over on the clean straw and felt the rustle of Mr. Tellison's letter in her bosom. She thought of his smile and his words, "Charlotte, I love you," and she wept bitter, stinging tears until she fell into an exhausted sleep.

At intervals during the long night, she awoke from horrible dreams of her burning home and the faces of her family floating before her. Down the passage she heard groanings and cries from the prisoners who, like herself, were experiencing similar apparitions. She wept afresh.

How she managed to survive the endless night, Charlotte couldn't remember. When morning pallor broke silent and gray, and a faint light funneled through the tiny barred window above her head, she heard clanking sounds coming down the passage with an accompanying grinding of keys. She sat up stiffly and strained every nerve in her body to detect the meaning of the early disturbance. It grew nearer and her breathing came in short spasmodic gasps. When the jailer came into view she cried out, "Did you get the message to Tellison Hall?"

"Yeah. Now come quiet like," he demanded. "I guess they didn't want to come fer ye."

Hesitantly she arose and clutched her parcel to her breast, trying to comprehend, to fathom the meaning of his words. They wouldn't leave her here—not like this—they WOULDN'T. "No! No. You don't understand; you went to the wrong House. No. . . ."

"Move. MOVE!" he shouted angrily.

When Charlotte stepped into the passage the man tore back her skirt from her ankle and attached a link of cold iron chain which, to her horror, connected to the long links that joined her to an endless blur of humanity already preceding her down the cold passage.

Ahead, a procession of prisoners was filing toward the stairway, each, like herself, dragging chains on his ankles and climbing the steps, straining to see where to place one foot and then the other, toward some destination unknown.

In the dim light, from the next story a voice shouted, "Move along with ye. Move along." And all obeyed as dumb beasts.

Somewhere beyond the pitiful column, a door was open and a chilling wave of cold salt air moved through the passage and engulfed the occupants shuffling forward and onto the cobbled shore toward a huge black fog-shrouded outline in the bay.

Seagulls screamed overhead and cold mists from the sea swirled about them. Soldiers stood with guns

62

pointed and ready for use in case one was foolhardy enough to hold back. From somewhere sounded a child's sobbing and a man's deep cough.

Charlotte was filled with such violent terror that she thought she would collapse. She wanted desperately to cling to the earth to keep from being put on that hideous black ship. When she pulled back, the chains jerked her forward. She stumbled, pitched forward, and clutched at the filthy rags of the man in front of her until she was pulled upright again. Her fingers grasped at her cloak to keep out the icy chill that stung every fiber of her being as she was forced along, step by agonizing step, toward the water's edge.

Up ahead a soldier shouted his threats. Mute silence prevailed and each surveyed his situation with an aura of hopelessness that defied description or reason. Each was dumb with fear of the unknown.

Beyond the soldiers, a crowd of people had gathered to watch the forlorn group parade from the molding jail to the vessel beyond.

"Be gone wi' ye, ye vile creatures!" yelled a woman. "Wicked sons o' Satan. Drownin' will be too good fer ye!" A surly woman picked up a clod of dirt and aimed the mass at a man in the front of the line. He received the forceful blow on his back and at once turned and slung vile railings in return. The crowd cheered and fell to slinging more clods for the sheer joy of hearing the filthy, angry retorts of the convicted man—taunted as a demented animal—poked, teased and tormented to blind fury.

Charlotte was filled with unfathomable shame to be counted among these criminals, marching past townsmen scattered along the street. She was a public spectacle of low degree, shuffling forward onto a rotting plank beyond bold gold letters on the ship's side that spelled out the name JUSTICE.

The prisoners were lined about the deck as the

ship's Captain and First Lieutenant, with legs apart, studied each one passing before them and tallied the numbers.

Charlotte was the last to move into their direct view. She felt the Captain's eyes devour her until she turned her head away in disgust. She was thankful that the Lieutenant had the decency to turn toward the railing to face out to sea.

When the prisoners formed a full circle about the quarter deck, the Captain came forward to address the group. He stood with his hands on his slim hips, feet apart, head high. "I am the Captain of this ship and I will expect to have orders obeyed or there will be dire consequences. Food will be brought to you upon settling in berths." Then he turned and stood as before to watch the soldiers herd the convicts to an opening where they moved forward and down a ladder into a low ceilinged area in the bowels of the ship.

The sailors were tackling the rigging with every ounce of strength for a fair wind had begun to blow and they were anxious to get under way.

When Charlotte's eyes fully adjusted to the darkness, she observed with numbed horror that a much larger number of prisoners had been in the ship before their arrival, and the stench of their bodies in the cold dampness told her that they had been in this position for some days.

The jailer came over to Charlotte, removed the ankle ring, and pulled her to an area where a group of women huddled together at the side of the hold near the ladder.

She leaned back to survey the lot in the light of the one lantern swaying gently on its peg by the ladder. It was indeed a sad, miserable gathering of humanity assembled before her and she wondered how long she would have to endure the confined company of the prostitutes.

The women studied Charlotte for some moments, whispering amongst themselves as to her origins and probabilities before one spoke out. "Yer a La-dy, ain't ye?"

Charlotte closed her eyes for she felt like anything but a lady right now. "It's not important," she whispered wearily without opening her eyes.

One of the women leaned so close that the rotten smell of her breath quite strangled the girl before she put her hand to her face to try to rid herself of the foul odor as best she could.

"Wha'ad ya do ta get in prison?" The woman poked Charlotte with her elbow and cocked her head.

"Nothing," Charlotte answered simply.

At this the woman gave her a sly smile and turned her head and body but not her beady eyes from the girl to view her with great derision. The black, scraggly hair stuck out bristly from her pale face and scalp and she placed a hand on her leg and sneered, "No-thin, she says. She ain't done no-thin." And the prostitute looked at the other women who mimicked her with pleasure. They all hooted and looked toward Charlotte.

Hot tears trickled out from Charlotte's closed lids and slid down her cheeks. She put her face on her knees. How much lower could she get?

On the boards across the narrow passage a boy of twelve drew himself into a ball and began to cry with great convulsive sobs causing several men to fling vile curses at him in hopes of putting a stop to the miserable display of emotion. The man beside the boy coughed and looked vacantly out into space through dull, lifeless eyes. He then rolled over onto his side and pulled his blankets about him to sleep.

The ship rocked nervously, rising and falling in a steady motion, and Charlotte knew they were underway, moving in a nameless direction out to sea, to some destination. Somewhere.

CHAPTER 5

TRUE TO THE CAPTAIN'S WORD, food was brought to them in the form of a thick oatmeal sweetened with molasses and served on a thin wooden plate. The mess looked good to Charlotte for she hadn't eaten for twenty-four hours past and was somewhat faint. No utensil accompanied the meat, and she lapped the food as an animal under the watchful eyes of the soldiers.

Later in the day, the jailer lowered himself down the ladder and walked over to Charlotte. From his waist, he produced a key and bent over her to remove the chains that bound her.

"Come with me," he ordered curtly. She followed him up the ladder with the prostitutes beneath bellowing out, "Be good to 'em, dearie!" and laughing at their own foul humor until the deck above thankfully drowned out their abusive remarks.

First Lieutenant Drummond, whom she was directed to follow, was slightly taller than she with a thick build and deep voice. He was courteous to her and, though he spoke no further word, the man appeared kind. They moved along the second deck until they came to the door at the end of the passage guarded by a soldier holding a rifle.

"We're to see Captain Blackmore," he said flatly. The soldier nodded, moved aside, and permitted the officer to knock.

"Enter," a voice called from within.

"The young woman, *Captain*," said Charlotte's escort with an added emphasis on the word, captain.

"Thank you, Lieutenant. Come in, Miss." He chose to ignore the cutting remark and nodded to the officer who stood hesitantly glancing at Charlotte and then at his superior officer before closing the door behind him. She was then motioned forward.

The captain's room was large, clean, and carpeted with a green color nearly extending to the walls. His massive table was well carved and polished to a high luster.

The man sat leaning back, refusing quite obviously to rise in her presence, feeling, no doubt, that she was unworthy of such a courtesy. He motioned for Charlotte to be seated before him. The tilted row of windows directly behind the captain cast a dull light on him as well as the bottle and two glasses that rested in front of him. His one eye lid drooped slightly, but he kept a steady gaze on the girl before him until she looked down with embarrassment to avoid the directness of his sinister eyes.

"What felony are you charged with, Miss Grey?"

"My employer falsely accused me of stealing a dish and keeping the money for it, sir."

"Falsely?" he quizzed.

"Yes, sir." And knowing that she was entirely guiltless, she looked directly, unfalteringly, at the man.

He put his hand to his mouth and rubbed the back

of his fingers absently across his chin while his eyes studied her. "And why do you say, falsely?" He proceeded to pour himself a drink from the wide bottle in front of him and calmly study the liquid in the small glass.

Charlotte gave the man a brief account of the events that led to her conviction and transport. He slumped slightly and rested his ankle on his knee while she spoke, but not once did he take his eyes from her body while she talked to him.

When she finished the account, he replaced his glass on the desk, rose, and walked slowly to the windows behind him to stare out over the sea. A great deal of time lapsed before he spoke again.

"The prison is not a pleasant place, is it, Miss Grey?"

"No, sir."

"It is no place for a lady. The filth, the rats. . . ."

Charlotte drew in her breath audibly and the man quickly went on with, "Oh, yes, Miss Grey, all ships have them between the decks. It's difficult to rid one's vessels of them, you know." He paused slightly then turned calmly to face her. "Do you read?"

"Yes, sir."

"And can you mend and sew perhaps?"

"Yes, sir."

"Again he fell silent while he began a slow pacing about her. Charlotte felt his odious, black eyes on her body, studying her.

"Miss Grey," he said softly, "I need someone to care for my linens and my mending and wait on me." By now he faced the girl directly and without taking his eyes from her face, the captain leaned on the table with a slight smile on his lips and said sweetly, "You will not have to live below deck, of course. You will enjoy perfect freedom on board ship, eat at my table, and spend your leisure time reading." And with this he pointed to his many volumes on the shelves lining the walls on either side of his room.

Charlotte's fear of the man began to rise as she sensed that his intentions toward her were anything but honorable. But before she could answer him, he opened the door and summoned her escort who was waiting outside in the passage.

"Tell the jailer that Miss Grey will be situated in my quarters, Lieutenant Drummond."

At the blatant statement, Charlotte rose swiftly and turned to the man. "I certainly shall not!" she cried out angrily. "Care for your linens, sew, and mend, yes. But sleep in your quarters, no!" And she attempted to run from him but the captain grabbed her arm until she winced with pain.

"On this ship, Miss Grey, you are my prisoner, and you shall obey my orders," he said softly but menacingly through his clenched teeth. A strand of black hair fell over the drooping lid as he talked.

"Then whip me and keep me in chains as it pleases you, sir, for I am truly, as you say, your prisoner. But I value my honor above life itself and what punishment you choose for me, I can bear it." And with this, she stood, firmly planted, and bit her lip rather than cry out in pain when his grip on her arm tightened almost beyond endurance.

By now the man was breathing hard while a look of utter contempt covered his face. "Put her back in chains," he snarled violently between clenched teeth. The captain threw her wildly from his grip into the arms of the lieutenant who put his arm about her and led her from the room. When the door closed behind them, Charlotte put her face into her shaking hands and leaned heavily against the wall to steady herself.

"It's all right, lass," she heard him say. "Come up on deck for a bit of fresh air before we go below." The man spoke kindly and soothingly to help her gain control of herself again.

69

When Charlotte looked up through her tears she whispered, "Where are we being taken, sir?"

"Why to be sure, lass, we're headin' for the colonies in America. You ain't been told?"

"No, sir."

The man took her arm gently and led Charlotte along the passage to the heavy ladder leading to the upper deck. She pulled her cloak about her; the wind was blowing with great sweeping gusts causing monstrous white capped waves to heave about the ship.

The bark was in full sail. Charlotte looked up in awe at the wind's work in pummeling the white canvas to full bloom and forcing the massive construction to pitch forward at such a rapid pace as if to appear entirely weightless.

Charlotte breathed in great gulps of the fresh, salt-spewn air into her lungs as if she couldn't get enough of it. She clung tightly to the railing and dreaded returning to the appalling darkness below. The lieutenant was casting anxious glances about the threatening sky and up into the masts where the seamen clung to their precarious perches far above the decks.

Lieutenant Drummond was a heavy, coarse man of perhaps forty five with black, greasy hair surrounding fat jowls and large ears. Beneath bushy, black brows, his dark eyes rested in deeply layered pouches. The space between his straight nose and upper lip was deeply furrowed down the center. The mouth, itself, formed a semicircle that curved downward over his teeth. But in spite of his gruff appearance and deep gravely voice, he was a man apparently capable of great gentleness.

The man drew his gaze back to the girl beside him. "We've a storm a brewin," he stated and glanced about again before turning to Charlotte. "Better go below."

The two turned toward the ladder once again as the

captain's head appeared from the lower deck. "What is the meaning of this?" the man stormed angrily. "Get below." And she obeyed with great haste.

When they approached the opening to the dungeon, Charlotte hesitated for a moment as the stench rose to her nostrils. "Sir," she said softly, "Is there no way to get more air down there?"

"The ventilator will have to be covered until the storm passes, lass, or the water will pour down on all of ye."

Charlotte nodded and turned to descend.

"The captain doesn't take kindly to bein' crossed and he'll try to pressure ye into submission."

"Then," said she, holding her head high, "he'll try in vain. My God will protect me, sir."

"Aye. Ye've got spirit, lass," he said. "Ye must have some sturdy Irish blood coursin' through yer veins."

"Thank you, Lieutenant, perhaps I do at that," she said and started below.

Charlotte's stomach retched at the fresh odors but she knew she would adjust somewhat. She crept to her small space and sat down to endure the storm as best she could, though she was apprehensive and extremely fearful. At best, she thought, a storm is frightful enough in a dwelling with four sturdy walls, but to be in a ship, tossed about like a cork. . . . And here she stopped, for a crash of ear splitting thunder resounded throughout the ship causing screams of fear amongst the prisoners.

The heaving of the bark on the great swells was causing havoc with seasickness. And the stench, with the vomiting, rose even viler than before.

The boy of twelve was still crying. Others were belching out vile cursing at the tops of their voices. Charlotte looked about her in horror at the ghostly sight caused by the dim light from the lantern along

71

with luminous fumes and she put her hands to her face in dread fright.

By now the rain was beginning to hit in great, pelting fury against the ventilator covering and deck. Each person tried his best to endure. Many were too sick to even cry out.

Charlotte sat huddled in her blanket and waited for the storm to take its course. "Oh, Lord," she pleaded, "we are chained to this horrible ship and will surely drown with it if it splits asunder. Keep us safe."

Just then a fresh bolt of lightning found its target near the vessel. She felt a small shock, followed almost immediately by a crash of thunder that shook the entire ship from bow to stern with its fury. The first peal of ear-rending thunder hardly ceased until another, even louder, split the air with such severity that Charlotte jumped involuntarily and pulled her blankets even closer about her. She beseeched her Lord to spare them from perishing at sea.

Overpowering fear ran through every thread of the woeful gathering. The storm raged on and each was stilled to utter silence in sudden and awful expectation of the vessel bursting apart, timber from timber. The water could surely converge in upon them to carry them to a watery grave with no chance of escape from their perilous irons.

Charlotte immediately stood and lifted both her face and her arms to heaven. "Oh, God," she cried out in the hearing of all, "Spare us from certain death and let our feet once more stand on firm ground. Keep us in Your care." Then, to the prisoners she admonished, "Ask the Lord Jesus Christ to come into your hearts and save you! Pray to your Maker!"

The sordid curses of many men and women alike changed to prayers as they faced the realization that they, in all probability, would face their Maker soon enough to answer eternal charges of earthly behavior unless God intervened. Men cried out to wives and children; boys to mothers to forgive them; others begged the Savior above to rid their blackened hearts of filth. And a general wailing prevailed.

Peals of thunder overlapped with those of a greater distance, in a rapid succession, and the storm raged on. Following one particularly violent blast, each nail in the seams of the ship lit up in unearthly succession about the prison before disappearing as swiftly as it began.

After a space of interminable length, of which they could only surmise, the woeful group sensed that the violent peals of thunder began to lessen somewhat and the bark lapsed into slightly calmer seas. The prisoners eased into likewise less anxious frames of mind. Charlotte felt calm assurance but called out a prayer of thanks – an audible thanksgiving for all to hear.

Many lay back and slept a sleep of complete exhaustion.

When Charlotte opened her eyes, she realized that the foul air had cleared somewhat and a sailor was descending the steps with a large basket in his arms. He began to pass cheese and biscuits among those who could eat and then returned later with a pail and dipper, allowing each prisoner one dipper full.

"That's half your ration for the rest of the evening," he warned the prisoners.

The water was a tantalizing torment for the few of those who could have taken much more but for most of the prisoners, the liquid added further unrest to unsettled stomachs.

The groaning increased to agonizing wailing and when she could stand it no longer, Charlotte put her hands over her ears to try to close out some of the inhuman misery about her. Realizing that seasickness was not going to overtake her, she closed her eyes and asked the Lord to undertake and relieve her fellow prisoners of their agony.

When the lieutenant lowered himself into the prison later that night, he informed Charlotte that the captain requested further audience with her. She welcomed any change to be better than what she now endured.

"The horror below is inhuman," she cried softly. "I'm so thirsty." And she leaned against the wall and put her hands to her mouth.

"Aye, lass, that it is," said the man with a sigh. Then he placed a reassuring hand on the girl's shoulder. "But I can help that a bit." He winked and produced a key from his pocket which he thrust into the next cabin door. He motioned her in. "Come along now; it's all right. Ye stand right there by the door for a bit."

It was a long narrow cubicle of a room built in the rear curve of the ship with painted boards running vertically from floor to ceiling. A narrow bed was pushed against one side and an old battered trunk rested against the wall at the foot. The lieutenant removed a squat bottle and glass from a space beneath a wash stand and after pulling out the cork, poured some of the pale liquid into the glass and handed it to her.

"It's sour so drink it slowly—all of it."

"Not spirits, sir?"

"No, lass."

Charlotte put the glass to her mouth and sipped the bitter blend of lemon and water until it was gone. It truly relieved her thirst but she thought of the poor wretches below and how they lay with parched throats begging to be relieved of thirst and finding no relief.

"Now we don't want to keep the captain waitin'," he said.

The two moved along silently toward the captain's

quarters. Outside the door he said, "There will be pressure, you can depend on it."

The captain was arranging papers on a side cupboard when she entered. Charlotte stood silently until he turned to face her. His studying of her resumed and the sinister smile appeared once again as he walked slowly and steadily toward her.

"Miss Grey, the storm was frightening, was it not, down in the prison?"

"Yes, sir," she answered, "but God kept us safe and delivered us." Charlotte let her eyes study the scene through the windows beyond him, refusing to look at his evil face.

The man passed slowly before her and circled her round about while lust filled his greedy eyes and eagerly devoured her.

"This prison is not to your liking, I presume?"

Charlotte refused to answer so he smiled and continued.

"These are lovely quarters, aren't they? Very airy, light and comfortable, wouldn't you agree?"

When she refused to answer the second time, he chose to ignore her impertinence and resumed his slow pacing.

"The smell is getting vile in the prison, Miss Grey?" he asked.

"Yes, sir. Very."

"Ah, well," he sighed. "Criminals must not be pampered, petted, and made to like their surroundings."

"No, sir, but we are human. I dare say your dog fares better."

"Ah, you do have a tongue, I see." And he sat down behind his writing table. "But dogs are obedient."

"As are humans if given proper treatment." With this Charlotte resumed her silence. Then the captain rose abruptly and heatedly added, "I have offered you excellent treatment, Miss Grey, but you continue to spurn my offer. You can be traveling as a lady if you choose." He came very near her, took her chin in his hand, and looked into her eyes.

"Perhaps you will change your mind." The captain would have kissed her had she not pulled sharply from his hold and moved toward the cabin door. But his quick movements thwarted any attempts at escape and she was once again in his vicelike clutches and entirely at his mercy. He remained a few moments behind her. She turned her face aside in horror while he continued to grasp her arms firmly in his hands and move his detestable body against hers, letting his face nuzzle the back of her neck.

Charlotte's flesh crawled at the touch of the creature's face on hers and when she felt his hands about her waist, she struggled so violently that he was compelled to release her with an agonizing twist of her arm that caused her to cry out in pain.

For some moments he leaned against the door and gazed at the girl. "You will come to me yet," he promised savagely. Then jerking open the door, he said to the lieutenant, "Miss Grey is disturbed with the prison odors. She has charge, hereafter, to rid it of those foul odors that are so distasteful to her tender nostrils. See that she does a thorough job and without help, Lieutenant." And with this, he held the door open while she slipped past and into the passage.

The pair walked slowly without speaking, but the officer knew she had won a second victory over the captain.

Charlotte asked for lanterns below so she could perform the tasks assigned to her. Lieutenant Drummond accompanied her and called loudly to the prisoners. "Miss Grey will give ye vessels. If a one of ye lays a hand on 'er, ye can lay in yer own filth.

Understand?" He stared at the group while they, in turn, knew what to expect.

Her task was to carry the disgusting vessels to the top deck to empty. It was a loathsome duty, but her heart ached for the miserable sufferers and she did it willingly. Somehow she received the strength from her Lord to make it up the ladders and down.

Charlotte kept at her duties while speaking to the prisoners about faith in God. Most of them were grateful for any little help they received, along with a kind word of encouragement.

One man lay very still. His thin face was grotesquely bony and his clothes hung in loose rags about his emaciated frame. "If he sleeps, he will do well," Charlotte whispered under her breath.

The lad of twelve looked up to her in the faint light with his large, terrified eyes and when she smiled at him, he returned a faint acknowledgment of her.

Late in the evening the wind increased. Charlotte stared out over the white capped mountains of water that lifted their bark up one side and tossed it forward down the other. Above, the black clouds swirled and permitted the moon only an occasional glance earthward. The air revived her somewhat but she longed to curl up on the deck instead of returning below to sleep.

She closed her eyes and leaned against the mast. A voice said softly, "Are ye well?"

"Yes, sir," she whispered. The two stood silently for a few moments and then she asked, "Is there water for bathing?"

"Aye. I managed to collect it from the storm and I've a kettle in my cabin and soap as well."

After bathing, Charlotte lay her head on her blankets and fell into a deep sleep that shut out the lewd, filthy talk and unrest that accompanied the night.

The following morning her entire body ached but she asked God for strength and resumed her duties. Slowly and painfully she picked up her blanket and made her way to the top deck. When her head rose above the ladder, she was greeted by a magnificent view of a glowing sun breaking through the soft gray clouds of morning. It cast a golden glory on the entire deck. Charlotte gasped in awe at the sight and stood entranced at the beauty before her; God's gift of splendor to a pathetic cargo.

From their perch high above the deck, the sailors cared little for the beauties of a sunrise and went about climbing nimbly up and down the rope ladders, hand over hand, with white canvas pants whipping about their legs.

As she neared the lower passages, a scream of horrible proportions reached her ears and she dashed down the ladder with the cursing jailer close behind.

The boy was straining at the irons about his ankles and pointing to the ragged man beside him. "E's dead, I tell ye,—e's dead." And the child burst into great fits of sobbing.

Charlotte tried to calm the lad, but her efforts were fruitless, for he took to gnawing on the back of his hand while the jailer did his examining.

"Fetch the surgeon," yelled the jailer.

Charlotte moved up the ladder trying to see through hot tears of anger at the horrible injustice of it all. "The man had probably poached a rabbit for a starving family or stolen bread rather than see his children die. Whatever the crime, it couldn't equal the punishment."

A murmur of deep discontent pervaded the room and the cursing resumed while the surgeon pronounced the man dead. The jailer unlocked the irons about his ankle and covered him with his blanket.

Charlotte painfully resumed her duties and shuddered at the thought of being buried in a watery grave at sea. But she kept her head up for surely the pathetic lot needed all the encouragement she could collect on their behalf.

It was after her second trip above that the jailer said, "Miss Grey, the captain 'as given orders for ye to sew up the body in the blanket. 'ere's the needle an' thread an' be quick about it."

Charlotte looked at the man and moved forward as one in a nightmare. "The vile creature will stop at nothing to get me to submit to his rotten passions," she whispered angrily. She knelt beside the body and pulled the blanket together to begin her stitching.

The boy reached his hand over and touched her arm. Charlotte turned to face the boy's frightened eyes and knew she must be strong. She was the only one of them free enough to move about and give any relief.

"It's all right," she said as she worked. "This won't last forever; just a few more weeks. We'll be free someday to begin lives for ourselves away from jails, and prisons, and captains, and then we'll forget these evils we endured for a time. We must keep up our courage. The best way is to ask Jesus Christ, God's Son, to come into our hearts. Have you heard of God's Son, Jesus?"

"No, ma'm."

"God sent His only Son to die for our sins. If we ask his Son, Jesus, to forgive us and live in our hearts," she said softly, "He will do it; I promise. He did it for me. He gives you peace. Then you have the strength to get through this. Ask him. Talk to him as you would talk to me, and see what He will do in your life."

"Then what're ye doing' 'ere if that's so?" asked a cynical man's voice nearby.

"Someone told a lie about me," she said calmly as

she worked on. "But God wanted me here. He has his reasons."

The boy continued to touch a fold of her skirt and he stopped his crying.

"Where are you from?" she asked him.

"London, ma'm. By the docks."

"Did you go to school? Do you know your letters?"

"No, ma'm."

"Why are you here?"

"I stole. But I would 'a paid 'em back. I told 'em I would."

"Well, you have food here and you aren't hungry now. You will have three meals a day and. . . . "

"Yeah and rot in this hole, that's what," said a man who'd been silent until now.

"It can't last forever," she reminded him quietly.

"We bin in this stinkin' hole for over two weeks now an' if there's no wind, we could be driftin' fer weeks afore we land again. An maybe it'll be worse under some master, that's what it may."

Charlotte chose to ignore the man and continued talking softly to the boy. "Have you a mother?"

"Yes and she carried on somethin' awful when I was took away."

Charlotte could tell that his eyes were filling with tears again so she said, "You can go back to her some day. Who knows. You may return a rich man. It's possible, you know, in the colonies."

When her task was finished, she nodded to the soldier. In due time two seamen carried the man out for burial and she wondered how many of the one hundred and twenty five of them left would set foot on that strange American soil.

CHAPTER 6

A FULL MOON SHOWN LARGE, and white as milk, illuminating the deck of the JUSTICE while one of the sailors cranked out lively refrains on a fiddle. The rest of the crew clapped in time.

As Charlotte took the last vessel to the railing, the lieutenant spoke to her from the shadow of the mizzenmast. "Is everything all right?" he asked.

"Yes, sir." She leaned against the gun rail and looked far out on the horizon. "I never realized there was so much water on the whole of the earth," she said wearily.

"And there's more t' come."

"How many weeks do you think we will be aboard ship?"

"Four more if we're lucky. Maybe five. Depends on the winds."

Charlotte sighed and stood with Lieutenant Drummond for a few moments.

"Why are ye aboard, Charlotte?"

"I wish I knew," she answered, "for I did nothing worthy of this sentence."

"Ye needn't tell me if ye'd rather not."

"It's a strange circumstance, sir." And she related her tale from beginning to end.

"Then ye had no trial at all?" questioned the man with alarm.

"No, sir."

"Ye loved the Tellison gent, didn't ye?" he asked gently.

"Yes." She whispered the word softly and sighed. Once again Charlotte remembered the warm touch of Ben Tellison's hand and the look in his eyes as he gazed at her. She wondered if she would ever see him again. It seemed completely hopeless unless God undertook for her.

A brawling noise below interrupted the tranquility of the night and her thoughts. Charlotte turned in horror. The fiddler continued playing as if nothing happened.

"It's all right. Just the captain and his companions. They're drinking heavy again tonight."

"I'd better go below, sir. I don't want him to find me here on deck." The noise from the captain's quarters grew more intense and she feared his door would be open so she crept rapidly down the passage to the lower ladder.

During the sixth week, much to the dismay of the jailer, one of the men developed a high fever with accompanying chills and headache. And when the surgeon was summoned, he came into the prison wearing a vinegar soaked cloth about his face. What he suspected was an accurate diagnosis. Smallpox.

The sick man was moved immediately to a section of the bottom deck away from the rest of the prisoners.

The surgeon ordered the convicts out of their berths and all able-bodied men were given the task of scrubbing the floor and walls of the prison with vinegar followed by several explosions of gun powder from the soldiers' rifles, to purify the air. Those prisoners who were left were herded out into the passage and ordered to sit beneath the ladder and about the area to wait until the floor was sufficiently dry to return.

The victim continued for two days with a raging fever, becoming delirious. He mumbled and shouted, calling, as was supposed, names and places of his shrouded past, until the last of his strength was spent and he cast about no more.

Instead of making the remaining one hundred twenty three more sober minded, the death had the reverse affect and somehow the hopelessness of their situation gave way to the lowest of filth in speech and action. Charlotte pleaded with the prisoners to turn their lives over to God. A few heeded her warning but most of the men and women ignored the plea.

For three days after the diseased man was buried at sea, the surgeon ordered lemon juice and fresh vegetables daily for each prisoner. The ventilator remained open at all times in spite of the weather and for a few days, the threat of the disease subsided.

The JUSTICE began its seventh week at sea and the prospects of landing in three more seemed a reasonable assumption had it not been for three days in which the wind nearly ceased. The seas became calm and the ship barely moved.

The officers drank to pass the time and the prisoners only desired more water.

By evening, Charlotte was extremely tired and felt warm and aching. The lieutenant wasn't at the gunrail as usual when she made her last trip to the top deck before retiring for the night, so she leaned against the rail and looked up at the starlit sky overhead. The air failed to stir so much as a wisp of her hair. As she looked out over the black waters toward England, she thought of Mr. Tellison and wondered if he sent for her the night he returned—if he discovered her absence and sought her whereabouts.

"No one saw me leave. It was such a strange parting," she whispered under her breath. "And yet, I can't account for my papers being sent along with my clothes." She sighed and a small tear slid down her cheek making a jagged path to her chin. Once again she felt the touch of Mr. Tellison's hand on her arm and heard him say that she did him good, that he loved her. "Shall I ever see you again," she whispered into the wind, "and know what it was that you intended asking me?"

As Charlotte leaned against the cool railing, she felt a chill through her entire body. Silently she made her way to the lieutenant's cabin and by the time she finished her bath, she was sick, and weak. At the end of the passage, the captain's door was open. She purposely hurried along to avoid an encounter with the man. But by the time she stood at the head of the ladder to get her breath, she saw the odious man coming toward her. She was too ill, at that point, to hurry away from him.

"Come here," the man snarled. "Where have you been?"

Charlotte could see that the captain had been drinking and she shrank from him with fresh revulsion. He was in an obviously restless mood but she was too sick to say a thing but breathe the name of her Savior.

"You brought a parcel with you and I want it. Now." Then turning toward Lieutenant Drummond standing silently in the passage near her, he spat out, "Get Miss Grey's belongings from the hold and bring them to me."

Why he wanted to inspect her parcel Charlotte

couldn't reason, but she leaned weakly against the wall to give support for her aching body while awaiting the lieutenant's return. By now she was becoming nauseous.

Lieutenant Drummond handed the parcel to the captain who immediately shoved his hand inside to draw out the contents, part of which tumbled to the floor. Charlotte tried unsuccessfully to retrieve the garments from the filthy floor and in doing so, reeled from dizziness.

"Aha!" gloated the captain. "So, you do own something other than the blue dress you wear so regularly." And he held up the flowered gown that Bessie had made for her.

"Put it on," he demanded.

"Please, sir," Charlotte pleaded faintly. "I am feeling sick."

"Do as I say!" he snapped angrily. "Come into my cabin to change." And Captain Blackmore took her arm and led her to a room next to the Great Room where he and the officers were gathered. With a turn of the key, the door opened and the man roughly pulled her inside. He hesitated, studied her full length, and went outside to wait for her.

By now the fever was rising and Charlotte ached over her entire body, but slowly she removed her dress, put the flowered gown on in its place, and leaned against the wall. "Oh, Lord," she whispered in anguish, "Help me. Please help me!" Silently she wept and the tears slid down the hot, feverish flesh of her face.

When the captain felt she had had sufficient time to change, he opened the door and found her with her face to the wall.

"Ah, that is a great improvement!" He moved slowly toward the girl while his greedy eyes studied her body. A faint smile played on his evil lips.

Charlotte desperately backed away from the man, but when she could move no more, he put his horrible hands on her and attempted to kiss her. She turned her face from him as he reached up and put his hand to the gauze about her neck. That act immediately caused her to shrink violently from his touch and leave the gauze dangling in his hand.

"So, my pretty," he crowed with pleasure, "there is more of you to delight me." And he grabbed her arm as she looked away in disgust. "The garments," he said as he forced her to face him once more, "can remain on my bed until we return later." And with a firm hold on her arm, he gave the gauze a toss without once allowing his eyes to leave her face.

The jailer appeared at the doorway in a drunken stuper. "Ah, there you are Captain. I thought we were to share this pretty thing but you keep her to yourself."

The captain scowled at the fool and snarled. "Get back to the other room."

The man was startled at the sharp redress and sobered slightly at the retort. "Yes, sir," he said and tottered unsteadily to the commanded location.

The captain turned to Charlotte and whispered, "Now my sweet, you shall entertain my men before I have you entirely to myself." And with this, he dragged the girl from his cabin.

The soldier at the door of the Great Room forgot his military dignity during the procedure and stared in stunned silence at the man dragging his stunning prize to the Room for all the occupants to gaze upon.

Everyone silenced while the senior officer stood her in the center of the room.

With great humiliation and shame, Charlotte let her head drop. Her eyes, hot with fever, closed. She could not bear to face the drunken fools in such a manner. The next thing the girl heard was the captain saying, "A toast, gentlemen, to the loveliest creature in all of England." And as he lowered his glass, he glanced at the fiddler saying, "Now you can play!"

The captain took Charlotte's arms and whirled her about the room. When the music stopped, she put her hands to her face, trying to maintain her balance. She vaguely remembered seeing the lieutenant by the window, gazing at her, then the room became black and she crumpled to the floor at the captain's feet.

When Charlotte came out of her faint, she found herself lying on the captain's bed while he paced the floor. She was much relieved to see that his door was open and that a lantern burned on a peg by the doorway.

At the first signs of movement from the girl, he came to the bed and looked down with a snarl on his face. "So. You made a fool of me with your act of fainting. But, Miss Grey, you are now my cabin guest and I shall see that you are duly humbled for I've put up with your impudence long enough."

Charlotte tried to rise but she was too sick to protest and fell back against the pillow to keep a wave of nausea from overpowering her. She put her hands to her face and closed her eyes.

"You needn't try to get away, Miss Grey. My guard is stationed at the door and will shoot anyone who tries to enter."

When the door closed softly, Charlotte grew numb with fear. Somehow she wrenched from his hold long enough to scream with all the strength left in her aching, feverish body.

Outside the door a loud noise was followed by a shattering of metal and a man came crashing into the cabin. The captain reeled in time to see the lieutenant brandish a knife at his face and, for a long moment, the two bent forward and faced each other with murderous hatred glaring from their black eyes.

"You'll hang for this, Drummond; I vow it—you'll hang," the captain snarled angrily.

"You filthy swine. Why my sister puts up with you as a husband, I'll never understand," hissed the lieutenant between clenched teeth.

The men moved about slowly as two wild animals in deadly combat.

Charlotte cowered with fear and looked up from the two long enough to see the soldier appear in the half open doorway. Instantly he lowered himself to his knees. He aimed his pistol at the same moment that the lieutenant lunged forward to deal a murderous blow at the captain's face. Charlotte screamed and the weapon fired.

The two men fell stunned to the floor while the bullet lodged itself in the girl's shoulder. Charlotte crumpled, bleeding and moaning, to the floor, in a state of unconsciousness.

For two days she tossed between consciousness and unconsciousness while her fever raged high at times and plummeted at others. When, on the third day, the fever dropped lower than it had been previously, she opened her eyes. At first she wondered why she wasn't in her own bed at Tellison Hall. The dark walls, low ceiling—where was she? And when she moved her arm, and it pained her, Charlotte realized that she was lying in some sort of a narrow bed.

"Is there much pain?" a voice asked softly from somewhere nearby.

"Yes, sir."

A cool hand felt her forehead and cheek. "Well, you are better. Much, I would say. But don't try to get up." He moved into view. "Now," said the surgeon, "you must eat something. I'll bring you some broth from the galley."

The man returned carrying a bowl of warm broth

and a spoon—a heretofore unseen luxury on this ship, she mused. The odors of the food made her realize just how hungry she was and Charlotte accepted the food with gratitude. Even before the spoon was put to her lips, she felt the flow of juices begin within her mouth.

"The ship is drifting, isn't it, sir?"

The surgeon raised his brows slightly and nodded. "Yes. It's been doing that for three days."

She sensed no alarm in his calm tones. "This is a usual thing at this time of year?"

"No, not usual. But we are entirely at the mercy of the winds."

"Yes," she said. "I suppose we are."

With another spoonful, the bowl was emptied of all liquid. The surgeon placed the spoon in the dish and put both on the basin against the wall.

"Sir, I had some coins and a letter on me. Do you know where they are?"

"Safe in the cloth. At the bottom."

Relieved to know that they were safe, she closed her eyes to drift off to sleep once more.

By the next day, Charlotte wondered how the prisoners fared, who the captain enlisted to carry on with her duties, and if the boy still cried. As for the lieutenant, she thought it strange that he hadn't been by to inquire about her. And where, she wondered, does he sleep if I have his bed?

When the surgeon returned she asked, "How are the prisoners?"

"A few boils have appeared but no new cases of pox."

"And the boy?"

The doctor shrugged. "What can I say? He cries less and his spirits have improved." The man bent down, took the squat bottle from below the lieutenant's basin, and poured some lemon juice into the glass. "Here. Take all of it."

Charlotte drained the glass. It puckered her lips and caused her to close her eyes slightly from the bitterness of it. "Where, sir, does the lieutenant sleep if I am occupying his bed?"

For a moment the surgeon didn't answer but then he said, "You mustn't worry about Drummond. He's provided for." He turned to arrange something, refusing to look at her.

"Where is he?" she insisted. When the surgeon didn't answer, Charlotte continued. Her fears rose with her voice and she struggled to raise herself on her one good arm. "The captain threatened him, sir, with hanging." Charlotte's voice trailed away into a whisper while her body shook with pain.

"Please lie down," the doctor ordered impatiently while putting his hand behind her neck to push her gently back down onto the bed.

"Only tell me where he is; please tell me." And the tears glistened in her pleading eyes. Her hand clung to his arm and clutched at his shirt.

"All right," he nodded firmly. "He is in chains but he is all right."

Charlotte closed her eyes. "In chains," she whispered. "The captain makes no idle threats, does he? But the lieutenant did it for me," she said facing the surgeon. "He came to my rescue. Surely the captain can understand that."

The man said nothing but walked to the doorway and gazed down the passage, his back to the distraught girl.

"When may I dress, sir?"

"As soon as the soreness disappears and the wound heals properly." Then turning to her he said flatly, "Now try to get some rest."

Charlotte stared straight ahead of her and wondered what the captain would do to the lieutenant. Threatening the life of a ship's captain would, no doubt, be an act of serious consequences.

During the long night, Charlotte slept fitfully—waking, dozing, dreaming of her past, fearing for her future, wondering about Ben Tellison—wondering, wondering. And with the first flicker of lantern light in the passage, she slipped carefully from her bed, pulled the cloth parcel from the peg, and groped her way along the wall until she made it back to the bed again. Without nausea.

Charlotte leaned back and rested for she was still weak. But she was making progress. Soon she would be able to be up and about.

She untied the knot and felt among the contents at the bottom. The precious letter was there. Her brush, the coins, the papers—all were where she put them and she breathed a sigh of relief.

"Oh, my Lord," she whispered, "There's so much I don't understand, and probably never will. Prepare a place in a home for me and whatever I must endure; give me the strength that I need for each day to bear it."

As Charlotte prayed, her fingers curled around the letter—Ben Tellison's letter—where it had fallen beside her. "Let him find me," she whispered. "Let him know where I am." And in the faint light of dawn she let the tears trickle to the pillow beneath her head.

When Charlotte raised her eyes, she realized from the uneven swaying of the room that they were moving once more toward their destination; a new land and a new life.

For the next two days, Charlotte tried to rest and gain strength but the lieutenant came to her mind frequently and she felt she must see him and learn for herself if he was well.

The voyage proceeded with the aid of strong winds billowing the sails in a westward course.

With warmer weather the surgeon ordered the prisoners to exercise more often on the deck. Charlotte was aware of the clanking chains as the feet of the inmates crawled the ladder upward to the light of day and abundant air for their stench-filled lungs. She cringed, from habit, at the shuffling feet and the accompanying mute silence of despair and degradation. From somewhere the captain shouted sickening threats. She wondered at the inner festering, the seething revulsion, that filled the souls of those who were made to parade before the man.

The surgeon brought Charlotte biscuits and cheese but when she broke a biscuit open, she found weevils crawling about inside and put it back down with disgust. *I'm so hungry,* she cried, *but I can't eat this. It's more than my stomach can accept.* She picked the mold from the cheese and ate it very slowly.

When the surgeon returned to the cabin, he saw the biscuits still on her plate. "We've yet one week or more at sea, Charlotte, and a few weevils when one is very hungry, should not cause you to waste food."

Charlotte didn't answer. After a few moments, she asked, "Have you made many trips across the ocean, sir?"

"Yes." The surgeon sat on the old trunk and leaned back to study her and answer her questions.

"What is it like in the colonies?"

He looked up at the ceiling with his hands propped by his sides for support. "There is much wilderness. The people live simple lives for they work hard to earn their bread. They're a people with passionate desires to be free. From what I can determine, England will not be able to hold onto this headstrong colony for it defies bounds. The people fight the elements to exist and they relish freedom. The planters feel strangled by import duties and forced debts imposed by the merchants they serve."

"Don't they relish the protection that England gives?"

"The colonists don't consider it protection. It's more like bondage, I'd say. When the time comes—and it will come—the people will fight to throw off that yoke forever." He pushed himself upright and looked at the solemn face on the bed. "But there is kindness to be found, Charlotte. They are a just people and believe that men are worth their toil."

"And what will become of us?"

After some moments the surgeon continued. "It is a little difficult to say. The women usually are taken to homes as serving maids. But come," he said rising, "you won't be able to even carry a tray if you don't eat. Finish your biscuits so you can keep up your strength. We have, you know, a week or more before that time." Then he smiled at Charlotte and turned quickly to depart down the passage.

The following morning, when the surgeon came into the cabin, he found Charlotte dressed and determined to go below.

"I think it best that you not go down into the prison just yet."

"But I must, sir," she insisted. "I owe so much to the lieutenant and I must see how he is."

The man sighed. "Very well, but you are to return to the cabin afterward for rest."

She made her way down the passage to the ladder and descended using her one good arm for support. The stench seemed to have lessened and when her eyes adjusted to the dimness of the room, she saw one of the women smiling.

"Thanks to you dearie, we been loosed and ordered to take over your duties. We come and go as we like." The women strolled the aisles with their brazen looks staring dully from beneath white lids.

Charlotte stood in silence. Then she saw the lieutenant. He was sprawled on the floor with his face on his blanket. His back, exposed to the lantern light, was covered with red welts. They were long, and ugly, and bleeding. She cried out and knelt down beside him.

"What has he done to you?" Charlotte put her hand gently on the man's arm. He barely opened his eyes to see who it was that spoke to him.

She looked at the boy chained by the lieutenant. "How long has he been like this?" she asked.

"Two days, ma'm."

"And the surgeon sees him?"

"No, ma'm. The captain don't allow it."

"Has he eaten anything?"

"Not much."

Charlotte glanced at the lad once more and then placed her hand on his arm. "And how about you? Are you well?" she asked.

The boy nodded but he still gnawed the back of his hand somewhat.

Charlotte rose quickly, ascended the ladder, and went directly to the surgeon. The man was in his cabin bent over the ship's diary when she entered.

"Sir, the lieutenant. . . ."

"Yes. I know. It's not a pretty sight but I'm forbidden to go near him."

"But I'm not," she said defiantly. "Tell me what to do and I will take care of it."

At this the man looked at Charlotte. For a moment he hesitated. "Very well, then. I'll get hot water. You wait here until I return and then you can go down and bathe his wounds."

"When was he whipped, sir?"

"Two days ago. The captain said it was an example to the rest who dared question his authority." And he hurried from the room to get the promised water.

Charlotte sat on the trunk and put her face in her hands. She wondered what the captain intended to do with his officer when they reached port. The contemptible creature was capable of unfathomable cruelty and she feared him greatly, wondering if anyone would come to her rescue if the need should arise again. She had not seen the captain since the shooting but she questioned how long that would last.

The surgeon returned and whispered, "I put the water by the lieutenant. Bathe his wounds until the water is cool and give him some broth when it is brought down to you. But take care. If you see the captain, stop immediately and pretend to do something else."

Lieutenant Drummond groaned and drew back when Charlotte touched a cloth to his sore back, but she continued as ordered until the water was cold. After she spooned the last of the broth into his mouth, he turned over and fell asleep once more.

"I'm glad you're here to watch," Charlotte whispered to the boy.

In the afternoon, the prisoners were taken to the top deck for an hour. It was the first that Charlotte had been in the fresh air for days and she breathed deeply of the salty sea air, filling her lungs, allowing the warm breezes to bathe her face and body in their softness. Eagerly she lifted her face to the sun for its warmth.

The lieutenant, she observed, was not one of the prisoners who enjoyed the partial freedom of the outing. His lot was to remain chained as a mad animal. How he was surviving the prison was a matter of conjecture for he gave no hint as to how he was enduring. No doubt he had strong thoughts on the matter but those thoughts were kept closely guarded from everyone including herself.

The next morning Charlotte found the lieutenant sitting with his back against the wall and his face in his hands.

"Good morning, sir," she said softly. "Let me see

how your back is healing. The man turned around as requested and smiled slightly but said nothing. While she examined him he whispered, "How many days until we land, lass, have ye heard?" His head was turned back toward Charlotte, but even though he could not see her, he strained to hear her answer.

"I have heard that we shall, with continued favorable winds, land in two days."

Lieutenant Drummond nodded but made no reply for a few moments. "Is there water left in my barrel?" he asked softly.

"Yes."

"How much is there? Will it last two days?"

"Yes, easily. I've been very saving of it."

"Then I'd like to shave if you will bring me soap, towel, strop, and razor."

"I will fetch them, sir." She hurried to his cabin and piled the requested articles in his basin.

After the shave, the lieutenant's spirits were improved. He talked to the boy with such a degree of humor that the lad laughed for the first time in eight weeks.

Charlotte returned the shaving equipment, hidden beneath her cloak, to the cabin. But when she put the articles into the cabinet, she discovered that the razor was missing from the basin. For a moment she froze. Why would he keep it? she wondered. What would he do with it? Is he so discouraged that he would harm himself? Knowing Lieutenant Drummond as she did, she doubted that that was the case.

She was so deep in thought that she didn't see the surgeon staring at her.

"Is everything all right?"

"I don't know," she whispered. "I took the lieutenant his shaving things but he kept the razor."

The man thought about her words before he spoke. "Drummond has a plan for escape. We'll have to pretend we know nothing, Charlotte. He is a just man and he's been ill used. Say nothing to anyone about this," he said quietly.

"Yes, sir. You can depend on me."

The following day the lieutenant was still in good spirits. Charlotte watched him carefully for she truly hoped, yes prayed, that in some way he could escape the fate the captain had planned for his ultimate punishment. She knew that if she were called upon to aid him in any way, she would do it. But the man gave no sign of a plan.

By noon the captain gave orders for the men to appear by two on the top deck in order for the ship's barber to transform their disheveled appearances into degrees of respectability. The application of the razor contributed somewhat to raising their spirits in their last hours before landing in Virginia.

Those who were fortunate enough to have a change of clothing, changed during the afternoon, for it was expected that the sighting of land would come within the next twenty-four hours.

The lad, by this time, developed an attachment for the lieutenant and no longer gnawed the back of his hand. "Look," he had told the boy, "you'll consume those hands if ye use them that way. Ye've got to be brave and face life as it is. Always do right, lad." And then the man spent hours telling the boy wild tales of the sea.

The following morning when Charlotte went below, Lieutenant Drummond whispered, "Will ye let me know when land is sighted and when we drop anchor?"

"Yes, sir. I will."

The prisoners were talking about the forthcoming landing in various degrees of enthusiasm. Some talked of returning to England while others talked of nothing but getting off the ship and planting their feet on dry soil once more. As for Charlotte, she had to pray against despair. Her sentence was for seven years. At twenty six she would be free—to do what? Would it be possible to return to Tellison Hall? Would Ben Tellison even remember her? Had he searched for her when he found her missing? And the boy—what would become of him? When his six years were ended, he would be but eighteen. He could return home to his family if he had the fare to go back.

After the noon meal, the prisoners were taken on top deck for their hour of exercise in the fresh spring breezes. Little was spoken—all eyes were strained for glimpses of land ahead or word from the sailors. Each tried to imagine his life begun without chains in a strange wild land far removed from his familiar English soil.

While the prisoners walked about, the soldiers gave their charges vacant looks and thought of a holiday in port, away from the miserable lot on board.

The captain held his eye to the spy glass that he kept pointed steadily in the direction beyond the jib. When he spotted a narrow sliver of hazy gray on the horizon, he broke into a grin. No doubt the thought of the money he would get for his cargo brought a touch of eagerness to his face.

The wind kept up its steady beating against the sails, pushing them toward the prized goal ahead. Charlotte watched the wind's work and prayed desperately that her terror wouldn't increase along with the patch of land ahead.

When the prisoners were seated in three rows around the foredeck, the captain came forward to speak. "We are now approaching the state of Virginia. We will continue up the bay to the James River and on to our destination. If any of you have entertained thoughts of running away from your masters, be assured that your names will be posted in public places and you will most certainly be returned to your owners. You will serve one extra day for each hour you run away and a full week will be served for a whole day's absence.'' He looked about him. The same vile sneer remained on his evil face.

"Oh, how I long to be rid of the man forever," Charlotte whispered under her breath. But she thought about his words as the land loomed larger and larger before them.

It was late in the evening before Charlotte fell into a fitful sleep, for the lieutenant complained of severe pains in his head and she was deeply concerned for his welfare.

The following morning blushed rosy and hot, and after the usual meal of oatmeal, the convicts were allowed on deck to watch the passing shorelines on both sides of the river. The air was cool and little wind blew.

The riverbank was edged with trees bearing foliage of deepest green which ran hard by the water's edge and was broken only by a clearing here and there on which stood a dwelling or a wharf.

Ships of varying proportions and sails passed by on the river in view of the JUSTICE. The waters were far spread and deep and seemed more like a vast sea than a river. By noon, the ship slowed in the black waters of the river and pulled to within seventy five feet of the north bank before dropping anchor. The sailors scuttled about the rigging while others secured the vessel for waiting off shore. Thus the vessel settled down to rest from her voyage of eight weeks.

During the afternoon, the lieutenant suffered from continued headache and developed some difficulty breathing. He soon began to thrash about and speak incoherently. When his voice became loud and boisterous, the soldiers sent word for the surgeon to come quickly to the prison. Immediately Lieutenant Drummond was ordered to the cabin where he could be under constant observation by the doctor.

The captain informed the prisoners that they would remain on board until morning for he would have to make arrangements with the authorities on shore.

Charlotte spent her remaining hours talking with the boy chained beside her—reading him scriptures from her papers and telling him of the love of God. He stopped his crying to listen to her tell of the strength and peace that Jesus gives and when she finished, he bowed his head and let the Savior come into his heart. His eyes filled once more with tears, but this time they were tears of joy. Charlotte clasped the boy in her arms and thanked God for His mercy and His hope.

The following morning everyone was awakened by the soldiers bursting into the prison. Guns were raised at the heads of the convicts and the captain faced the prisoners.

"Search for him!" he screamed.

A hush fell over the group and each stared at the captain in silence. The soldiers shoved the prisoners, jabbed them unmercifully with rifle butts—cursing, searching every space. When the captain moved toward Charlotte and the boy, he sneered in a loud hate-filled voice. "Where is the lieutenant?"

Charlotte eyed the vile creature with contempt. "He was delirious so the soldiers moved him to another place but I don't know where."

"What did he say to you last evening?"

"That he had a headache."

"And that was all? Surely you lie!"

"I tell you that I do not!" she cried angrily, looking him directly in the eye.

The captain paced the floor then turned suddenly and, with the soldiers following, flew up the ladder.

"Aye! The lieutenant got away!" laughed a ragged man. And the jubilant retorts began running across the entire prison.

"He had a headache, did 'e?" they laughed.

"E's a smart one, 'e is, an prob'ly miles off in them woods by now!"

"Bein' et by savages out there."

"E 'ad to swim a piece last night."

"If 'e got off the boat, I'd say. I know what I'd do — I'd swim fer it, I would."

"An be 'anged fer it later?"

"They'd 'ave to catch me first!"

The prisoners whooped and laughed and felt generally jubilant at the thought that one of them could escape from under the nose of the vile captain and his soldiers.

Could it be possible, thought Charlotte, that he did get away from the captain and the ship? If well wishing could strengthen bold endeavor, the lieutenant would be far away indeed for every man in the jail placed himself as a David fleeing his Saul.

From her view of the town that morning, Charlotte thought of the dark waters separating the ship from the shore and tried to determine the length of time that it would take a man to swim from the JUSTICE to the far shore in the dead of night with total darkness. Somewhere, she thought, he has taken refuge by now. But she was sure that the captain would post his name with the authorities in the port town and search him out as the hounds do a fox. Charlotte sincerely hoped that he would not be found. "Lord, wherever he is, keep him safe," she whispered.

The captain and the soldiers continued their intensive search for about forty minutes before the ship moved silently toward the shore and maneuvered alongside a timber dock extending beside the town's edge.

Instructions were sent below for the prisoners to tidy themselves. Each clung to his worldly possessions in anticipation of some action near at hand while the jailer unfastened the irons.

It was mid morning before Charlotte talked to the surgeon. He was tired and weary but managed to stop a moment to speak with her.

"What of the lieutenant?" she whispered.

"Don't worry," he admonished her. "If he made it to shore, he has friends in town who will take him in. He's as well liked as the captain is hated. No officer of the law will aid in the search for him—not really." Then he stood for an instant and looked at the girl standing before him.

"Good luck, Charlotte," he said softly. "May God go with you."

CHAPTER 7

ALONG THE WHARF, curious onlookers gathered to stare first at the black ship and its strange cargo and then at coaches halting and discharging gentlemen who made their way onto that ship to do business. The captain had already set up a small table with records and quills for the tallying of sales.

Charlotte found it difficult to know just what to do with her eyes during the process for it was a humiliating thing for her to be viewed, and searched, and poked, as a man would bargain for an animal. From where she stood, she watched the gentlemen taking the younger, stronger convicts to the table of business and argue until they were satisfied that they got the best bargains for their money.

After some time, a surly looking individual walked slowly by in front of Charlotte and stopped. "Turn around," he demanded roughly. She turned as bidden but whispered a prayer for God to work out His will in this matter.

"What trade?" the man barked.

"Housekeeper, sir."

"What is your conviction?" The man's eyes pierced hers as splinters of glass.

"Stealing," she said flatly—"falsely."

He apparently did not believe Charlotte for he shot her a look of contempt and passed on. Thankfully. The man moved along the whole line of prisoners before stopping directly in front of the boy of twelve. He turned him around in the same manner as he had Charlotte.

"Your name?"

"William, sir."

"Walk to the railing and back, William." The boy stood tall, threw back his shoulders, and marched as a soldier on parade. Charlotte was astonished at the complete change in the lad.

"M-mn. Open your mouth." The man proceeded to put his disagreeable face near the boy's to make his critical search of the state within. When he had felt William's arms and legs, the surly fellow instructed the boy to wait by the tallying table while he continued on to inspect the adults.

William stood straight and tall and looked directly at Charlotte. A smile appeared on his face and he nodded ever so slightly as if to say, "It's all right, Ma'm. I can take on anything now that Jesus goes with me."

Charlotte returned the smile, nodded likewise, and prayed silently. "Keep him, Lord, for he's Yours now." Deep in her heart she felt a surge of thanksgiving to accompany the glistening tears forming in her eyes.

Two gentlemen approached the women while Charlotte's eyes intently studied the lad. One was an older man, plump, bearded, well dressed in a black suit, and remarkably resembled the younger man in appearance. His manner was the same but he appeared the quieter of the two.

"Well, Martin," the older whispered, looking at Charlotte, "I fancy this one trainable and alert for your mother."

"No, Father, it would not do. You know your failing and I suspect that this one would show spirit."

"But she is clean looking."

The younger man shrugged and moved on. "Trouble, Father, trouble."

The older man was unconvinced but he moved along with his son and took the liberty of casting one parting, hungry glance her way before disappearing from view.

By late morning, a number of the prisoners had been sold and Charlotte began to wonder what would become of her. For a few moments she leaned against the mizzenmast and looked wearily out over the wharf to the town beyond. The depth in which she concentrated on the view made her unmindful of a slender man coming aboard. He sauntered between the rows of prisoners until Charlotte looked up suddenly to see the fellow standing directly in front of her.

She folded her hands and lowered her eyes in embarrassment while he concentrated on the girl before him. For some time the man glanced the full length of her then moved quietly toward the railing to think before coming to a decision. Finally he asked, "What is your name, Miss?"

"Grey, sir. Charlotte Grey," she answered softly.

The slender man nodded slightly and pursed his lips together tightly before he continued in an easy manner to question her further. "How many years are you to stay?"

"Seven, sir."

"And the cause, Miss Grey?" he asked quietly while searching her face for the answer.

"I was, sir, accused of stealing a dish and keeping the money." Her answer was direct and straight forward but spoken softly.

"Accused?" he asked leaning forward, turning his face slightly, but not his eyes, from the girl.

"Yes, sir, for it was done falsely." And she raised her face to look directly into his eyes while the wind blew wisps of pale hair over her brow.

The man turned his gaze away and took a few steps while concentrating and considering her response to his questioning.

"What type of work are you suited for?"

"Housekeeping, sir."

"Can you read?"

"Yes. Very well, sir."

He studied her face once again while his hands rested behind him. Then suddenly he wheeled about and strode over to the table where he immediately engaged himself in conversation with the captain.

After a few moments, the captain turned his face and looked directly at Charlotte while he spoke. Upon finishing with the words that he had to say about her, the senior officer watched the man take a small money pouch from his pocket and hand him the asking price of her. Immediately the fellow came and claimed her as his legal possession.

"My name is Mr. Blighton, Miss Grey. I am the steward of Flaight Plantation."

Charlotte followed the man down the planking and along the wharf to where a long flat boat lay anchored to the dock. With a nod of his hand, four black men scurried over the side and into the vessel, taking places on the seats, and grabbing oars from the bottom of the boat. Mr. Blighton helped Charlotte to a seat and took a place beside her.

She gave one parting glance toward the ship and then studied the surrounding foliage crowding against the shoreline for as far as eye could see. Somewhere Lieutenant Drummond was hiding. Charlotte hoped that he made it to shore and was now with friends who would help him to escape the captain's clutches.

The small craft moved out into the black waters of the James River. At first Charlotte was frightened for the vessel was low in the water. When she looked over the sides, it seemed to her that there was no bottom to the depths of the river beneath them. She held onto the seat until her knuckles turned white. Charlotte watched the men's arms and backs move in rhythm with even, powerful strokes that advanced the boat, with the current, at a great speed up the river.

What a different journey this is from the one just nine months ago, she thought to herself. Her mind drifted to Mr. Tellison with his droll smile and sparkling eyes. She wondered if he ever gave her a thought. If, when she didn't return, did he have the same feeling of loss—of emptiness—that she felt for him?

Charlotte bit her lip to check the teary mist that threatened to form in her eyes. Purposely she turned her face toward the shoreline. She MUST believe that God had His hand in all of this.

Her eyes studied the woods while she wondered what kind of a house she would live in here in this vast wilderness. And what kind of master and mistress would she be working for?

Charlotte thought about Madam Tellison and pictured in her mind the woman's slow pacing and the final treachery. "Oh, Lord," she whispered with a catch in her throat, "help me not to hate the woman for what she did to me. Help me to learn to forgive—and forget."

Mr. Blighton seldom looked up during the trip. He spent long stretches of time studying the same papers before he turned from one page to the next. Charlotte stole quick glimpses of him when his head was bent low. The man was good looking and about thirty two years of age, of medium build, with blond hair laying in waves about his face. His eyes were pale blue. He seemed kind as well as calm.

At intervals they passed by vast stretches of fresh emerald fields. In others, cattle roamed aimlessly to enrich the soil and fare on rich green pasture. Here and there was a house of fair proportions. Black skinned men worked in steady rhythms cutting trees and sawing them into workable pieces. Charlotte wondered about the crops and, as if Mr. Blighton understood her questioning expression, he looked up, glanced first at the girl, and then at the fields before he spoke.

"The land along the river is tobacco land." He motioned with his head in the direction in which she stared then let his eyes go back again to his papers. She studied the land and recalled the words of the ships' captains at the Christmas dinner. Wasteful spendthrifts, were the exact words used to describe the planters. She wondered about those words. Were these farmers really what the captains claimed they were—wasteful spendthrifts?

The boat skimmed along in the water for so many miles that Charlotte began to wonder if they had left the end of civilization behind and headed to nowhere. She sincerely doubted that there was a sizable house of any kind this far from the seaport.

When she noticed Mr. Blighton folding his papers and sitting upright, she sensed that they were approaching their destination. The men aimed the boat closer to the shore and when Charlotte turned in her seat to watch, she saw it.

The house stood at the top of a gradual rise of land that began at the wharf and sloped upward in a carpet of green. Huge maples, oaks, and towering elms shadowed the lawn.

"Welcome to Flaight Plantation, Miss Grey." The steward smiled and offered his hand to steady her when she stepped from the boat and onto the landing.

The house was brick. In the center was a white

door. Windows on both sides and in the story above were arranged in a pleasing, symmetrical pattern. The roof contained six dormers and at each side of the house, brick chimneys rose well above the roof. Although the entire house was small compared to Tellison Hall, it was attractive in its simple beauty.

"Come along," Mr. Blighton said quietly. They trudged up the slope and entered the house by the front entrance facing the river.

"John, inform Mr. Flaight that I would like a word with him."

"Yes, suh." An elderly black man nodded and walked to a room at the end of a short hall.

"Wait here in the passage and we will send for you, Miss Grey. Be seated, please."

Charlotte nodded. The stuffed couch felt wonderfully civilized after the hard boards of the ship.

The house was well constructed and possessed a sturdiness and well ordered simplicity about it that caught Charlotte's fancy, but her concentration was not at present on the structure so much as on the voices coming from a room at the end of the hall. The one voice recognizably belonged to Mr. Blighton.

"Sir, you can trust my judgment on this matter," he insisted.

"But a convict, Blighton, whatever made you do it? I have to think of Maryanne. We won't be able to. . ." His remark was cut short when the two men came from the room and into the girl's view before the master caught sight of her. ". . . trust her with a th—" Here the man came face to face with Charlotte while she sat silently with her hands folded into a tight little knot in front of her. At first the master stopped short and simply stared at her.

"Mr. Flaight, sir, this is Miss Charlotte Grey."

The older man nodded in acknowledgment of her presence but she did not offer him her hand. She simply returned the nod, looking into his eyes for a moment, and said, "Sir."

"Lodge her in the carriage house, Blighton, for we have no other accommodations." With this remark, Mr. Flaight left them to work out the details of the girl's duties.

"Allow me, Miss Grey," said Mr. Blighton. He leaned forward to pick up her parcel. From the front door she followed him across the yard to the carriage house behind the main Hall.

The apartment to which the man led Charlotte was at the end of a great room that housed two carriages. It was a small dusty room with a bed, candle stand, a coarsely braided rug on the floor, and a fireplace that had not been cleaned from the last occupant.

"I'm sorry, Miss Grey. Had I known it would be occupied I would have had it cleaned."

"Sir," she said softly, "don't apologize." Her eyes filled with tears. "After the ship's quarters it will be delightful. I shall clean it thoroughly myself. But for now, may I have some soap and hot water, please?"

"I'll send Annie to bring you a basin. There's water in the well just outside the coach house." Then he turned to go but before he closed the door behind him he called back over his shoulder, "Better bolt the door tonight."

"Thank you, sir, I will."

One window located on the east wall afforded Charlotte some light from the overcast sky of midafternoon. She opened the door, pulled the rug from the floor, and took it outside to beat it as thoroughly as she could with an old cornbroom she found inside the carriage house. While she worked, she looked for the well. The thought of having all the water she wanted was a blessing indeed!

A black woman came from the back entrance of the house and walked toward Charlotte. "M'am, here's yo beddin.' "

110

Charlotte followed the woman into the room where she placed a folded cloth, soap, towel, basin, and sheets on the wooden bed frame. She put her small hand out to the woman and squeezed Annie's hand in her own. "I'm Charlotte," she said.

By the time the sun set, Charlotte had a clean, cozy room, her clothes were washed, and she had bathed. The only other dresses that she had were the flowered one and the emerald. She put on the blue dress and adjusted the gauze shawl about her neck.

She ate her evening meal with the servants. They sat near the fireplace in the great kitchen which was a red brick dwelling to the side of the house. From a huge, black pot, everyone took a bowl of stew that smelled delicious after the many cold meals at sea.

"Now yo eat up," admonished Annie. "yo is all skin 'n bone, chile."

As Charlotte ate, she glanced at the dark faces studying her. Did they, too, come as prisoners? she wondered. Did they have a captain as vile as Captain Blackmore and a ship like the JUSTICE?

John, the butler, was dressed in livery but the rest of the servants were clothed in a coarse blue fabric. Each had white cloths about his head and middle.

After supper the women tended to the dishes and silver that had been brought from the main part of the house. To make herself useful, Charlotte dried the utensils and put them on the table for transporting back into the family dining room.

Mr. Blighton stood unnoticed in the doorway. How long he had been observing her she didn't know, but Charlotte saw him motion her to a seat in a corner of the kitchen when he caught her eye.

While they talked, the steward studied the girl seated across from him. Her pale hair shone in the last rays of golden dusk sifting through the window. Her eyes met his with a straightforward purity that he had

111

seen in few others. He thought to himself that he had made a good choice and that he would not regret it.

"The master's name is Martin Flaight," he told Charlotte. "He has a daughter, Maryanne, who is sixteen. Mr. Flaight is a widower so the two make up the family here at the plantation. The girl has a governess, a Mrs. Langley, but we have been without a housekeeper for four weeks now. Continue to take your meals with the servants and sleep in the carriage house. In time, well, we will see what happens." Then Mr. Blighton rose and smiled faintly before he left.

When Charlotte returned to her room in the carriage house that evening, it was clean and neat and on her bed lay a fresh mattress filled with sweet-smelling straw. A blanket was carefully folded at the bottom.

Since she wasn't sleepy yet, Charlotte filled the basin and tub with water—feeling the luxury of taking all she wanted—and washed her hair. After fluffing it dry with her towel, Charlotte knelt and thanked her Heavenly Father for delivering her from the wretched chains of bondage and placing her in a decent establishment once more.

From her bed, Charlotte's eyes stared into the starry night. She wondered what Ben Tellison was doing right now and wondered if he gave any thought as to where she was or to what she was doing. Would they ever meet again?

Charlotte sighed wearily and closed her eyes but she felt the rolling of the sea even yet. In spite of it, she wouldn't complain. At least she was on land, clean, and her stomach was full for the first time in two months.

"I will not permit Miss Grey to handle our affairs," the master flatly told Mr. Blighton. He shoved the last of the cornbread into his mouth and looked out the window at the pale streaks of dawn coloring the eastern sky gold.

"Very well, sir, then it is satisfactory to let her clean. And I must add, she does a very thorough job of it."

"So be it then, but no more. I've instructed Mrs. Langley to keep Maryanne away from her at all times."

"That is hardly fair to Miss Grey."

"Fair!" exploded the master. "Fair! I refuse to have her influence my daughter in any way and the best way to do it is to keep her well out of the child's sight."

"As you wish, sir."

"I WISH!" said Mr. Flaight with a final, emphatic end to the matter.

The conversation was fully audible to Charlotte while she scrubbed the passage floors. "I am thought venomous," she mused. But after the encounter with the captain, she was happy enough to have the man ignore her if she had ANY choice in the matter.

In spite of the master's feelings about her, Charlotte was content in the household. She had a friend in Mr. Blighton who treated her with the greatest cordiality and respect and who often passed compliments her way while encouraging her to be patient.

How am I, she thought dryly, *to be otherwise?*

After the master's breakfast table was cleared away, John slipped into a chair by the kitchen table and had his meal with the rest of the servants. He was a tall lean man with graying hair and had, no doubt, been with the household for a long time. Seldom did he open his mouth but this morning he had a piece of news that was of interest to all.

"Tis said," John began, taking another mouthful of cornbread, "dar is a man on a convict ship done got away."

Charlotte's heart raced within her and she tried hard not to show her extreme interest but she had to ask, "How did that come about?"

His mouth was full but he proceeded in spite of it. "Was on a ship at da port and got away at night."

Annie and Lissy looked at one another silently from their dish pans. Charlotte tried to keep her eyes on the cloth and the dish she was drying, but she had to find out more.

"Were they looking for him?" She put the dish down to take another.

"Uh huh." John nodded in his slow deliberate manner and finished his meat.

"Did they have his name posted in a public place?"

"Don' know, ma'm."

"Did they find the man?" Charlotte queried further.

"No. Not afta a week. Da cap'n warns da peoples look out fo da man."

"He ain't come dis far, does yo think?" asked Annie.

"Don' know."

"How did you hear about it, John?" Charlotte asked. She stacked the dishes for him to carry to the dining room while listening intently for the answer.

"Mistah Blighton hears it from da town." The man leaned forward and put his arms on his legs to stare at the rising dawn beyond the river.

So, thought Charlotte, *this is good news. The lieutenant was not found and the captain had to sail away without him.* She drew, within her mind, a picture of the captain searching at the public places and about the streets at night, and speaking in enraged tones with the local sheriff. Charlotte hung her wet towel over a line by the fireplace to dry and seated herself on a stool.

"What would they do with the man if they caught him, John?"

114

"Hang 'em."

"I see," Charlotte said softly. She thought she had asked enough questions and thus remained silent.

The slaves gathered around the table to continue mending. Charlotte put her reddened hands on her lap and felt the papers that she had put in her pocket before leaving the carriage house. She took them out, looked at the faces about the table and said, "I have some papers that I want to share with you." But before she could unfold them, Annie looked up in surprise and stopped stitching.

"Yo reads, Miss Charlotte?"

"Yes."

Annie jumped up from her work and walked over to the fireplace where she carefully removed a brick and brought out a neatly folded paper. With it in her hand, she walked excitedly to the girl and placed it before her.

"I's had it a long time and wants ta hear it." She had that sparkle of joy in her black eyes that Charlotte hadn't seen since the last time she was with Mr. Tellison.

Charlotte looked at the worn pages of coarse paper and discovered that they were from a Bible. Where the paper was folded, the words had been pitifully worn away from much handling so she unfolded it with great care. When the creases were sufficiently pressed open in order to make reading legible by the early light, she proceeded to read.

"For God so loved the world, that he gave his only begotten Son, that whosoever believeth in him should not perish, but have everlasting life."

Before Charlotte could continue she looked at Annie bending over her mending and she saw a tear— a great, watery tear—slide slowly down the woman's fat cheek and drop unceremoniously onto the blue fabric beneath her needle.

115

"Ah hears it, oh, ah hears it," she kept whispering.

Charlotte's voice was shaky when she spoke. "Do you understand the words, Annie?" she asked softly.

"He lubs me, Miz Charlotte, He lubs Annie. He lubs all da slaves if'n dey ask Him. He lubs m' old papa an' mama. Oh, He lubs us." And she rocked back and forth and stopped her mending for she could no longer see it in her dark hands.

"Oh, Lord," Charlotte wept, "You've given me a true friend far from home. The first true friend I've found."

Charlotte read all the words that were legible and then read from the papers she had in her pocket. "I'll ask Mr. Blighton if we can read from the big Bible in the drawing room," she said.

"Oh, Miz Charlotte. God done bringed yo here," was all Annie could say.

The following week Mrs. Langley passed by Charlotte without so much as a nod. She was black-robed, stern, and straightforward. Her purpose was to have a word with the master.

"I have a letter stating that my sister—my only sister—is sick and I want to go to her. The planting is well enough along that Annie could supervise Maryanne. I simply must go." She stood tall and unyielding before the man.

"Very well, Langley. But," he added sternly, "if you want to be pensioned, I'll arrange it."

"I shall return, you can be sure of *that*." Thus speaking, she bustled by Charlotte once again, casting a look of contempt on the girl scrubbing the floor. She marched up the stairway to pack a few belongings.

Some time elapsed before a girl of sixteen followed the governess to the rear door. She waved her hand to the disappearing figure in the coach but received no acknowledgment whatever in return. Maryanne walked silently onto the front step, studied the brick building used by the steward, sighed, and walked back inside. As she started toward the office at the back of the house, Maryanne turned slightly. With interest she watched the new servant scrubbing the floor before continuing on.

Charlotte rose from her position long enough to wring the water from her rag and discover a pair of large brown eyes staring at her. She smiled at the girl and received the slightest touch of a smile in return. While she watched Maryanne, she saw her turn and melt into the end room to speak with her father.

Miss Flaight was put under the supervision of Annie as Mrs. Langley had suggested, but the arrangement was anything but satisfactory for Annie. The woman had her own work to do. The girl desired the companionship of her father and spent many hours at his heels until the man completely despaired of the whole thing.

Mr. Blighton boldly approached the master after a particularly trying day with the daughter and the fields as the culprits, trying his thin patience sorely.

"Langley may be gone for months, Blighton," said Mr. Flaight.

"True enough." The steward paused slightly then added, "and so you really cannot hire a replacement for fear Mrs. Langley will return and be indignant."

"No, I can't. That's the devil of it." He moved uncomfortably in his seat. "Maryanne's underfoot all the time." Then he arose in somewhat of a passion and paced the floor. Suddenly he turned and faced Mr. Blighton. "I can't get my work done."

"Well, you have an alternative."

"I can't see that I have any at all." He leaned against the marble mantlepiece and put his hand to his mouth before he began pacing again. He sighed and absently rubbed his chin.

"But you do."

"Do what?"

"Have an alternative, sir," said Mr. Blighton quietly.

The master stood with his legs apart, hands behind him and asked, "What?" The man really did not expect an answer.

"I have been listening to Miss Grey read and sing to the servants and. . . . "

"NO!" he shouted. He glared at his steward and with a forced, spitting whisper added, "I don't even want her in the house." With this he was a little subdued.

"True, sir, you do not. But, she is here nevertheless. And I tell you truly that she is educated—a truly well-educated young woman."

"And a thief."

"No, sir, she is not. But then that's something you will have to find out for yourself."

Mr. Flaight seated himself once more and dejectedly picked up a paper from which he read nothing whatsoever before throwing it down on the desk unread.

"All I ask is that you have an interview with her and speak with her. You have, so far, completely avoided her."

"That's my affair, Blighton."

"So it is. But it is, sir, an alternative for just as long as Mrs. Langley is gone. What harm could possibly come under your own roof?"

The master closed his eyes and leaned back wearily in his chair. Finally he looked at the ceiling and said quietly, "I'll not do it. Now that's the end of it."

Mr. Blighton sighed and left, but he had a smile on his face just the same.

CHAPTER 8

BEFORE CHARLOTTE PUT HER FINGERS into the pail of strong lye soap, she cringed with pain. Her hands were red and sore from hard use. Even so, she thanked God that she had a decent place to live. She started scrubbing the rear entrance to the house when John's voice startled her with his announcement.

"Da mastah wish ta see ya."

Charlotte quickly finished the remaining section of floor and rose to empty the water. She attempted to make her appearance as neat as possible before appearing at the library door.

"Sir," she said without emotion. Charlotte had no pretense of pleasure at the sight of the man sitting at his desk.

"Come in," Mr. Flaight said with barely a glance in her direction.

Charlotte moved forward but kept herself a fair distance from where he sat at his work. He neither asked her to be seated nor did he invite her to come closer so she stood erect, with her hands folded before her, and looked directly at the man studying a book in front of him.

Martin Flaight was a tall, powerfully built man of forty. There was little refinement about him and even less beauty. He did possess a great abundance of energy that accounted for the fact that he was able to manage a prosperous livelihood in the midst of so much wilderness.

The man moved sideways in his chair and put his hand to his mouth but he kept his eyes on his book until he spoke. "You read, Miss Grey?"

"Yes, sir."

"Play the harp and harpsichord?"

She nodded slightly but affirmatively.

The man's eyes glanced the full length of the pretty girl for a fleeting moment before he turned away and continued. "My daughter's governess has left for awhile and I don't know when she'll return. It may be soon." Mr. Flaight straightened but kept his eyes on his book. "Could you work with her?"

"I will try, sir."

"Then begin in the morning." Without further ceremony the master set about his work and refused to acknowledge her presence another moment.

Charlotte turned from the man, but she felt at ease, sensing that they met on somewhat equal ground. She did not particularly desire to talk to him while he, on the other hand, seemed shy around her for some reason or other.

For the remainder of the day, she moved as far along with her scrubbing as she was able. When her pails were put away, she could do so with a sense of visible accomplishment to her credit.

After breakfast the next morning, Mr. Blighton took Charlotte into the drawing room to meet Maryanne. While he talked to them both, Charlotte noticed that the younger woman did not once take her eyes from the young steward from the time he first walked into the room.

After the ceremony of introductions was over, and the two young women were left alone, Charlotte felt Maryanne stare at her suspiciously without opening her mouth. Charlotte prayed for guidance in dealing with the girl for she had the feeling that Maryanne was strongly influenced in her opinion of her by both Mrs. Langley and the master.

"Would you care to go for a walk with me, Miss Flaight? I have not seen a plantation and I'm interested in watching the operation in the fields.

"If you wish," Maryanne answered softly but flatly. The girl was small and pretty with thick chestnut hair formed into fat curls at the back of her neck. Her eyes were the same dark color and sparkled brightly only when Mr. Blighton was around.

"I'll go downstairs for my cloak and meet you at the foot of the stairs," said Charlotte.

Maryanne nodded and also went to her wardrobe for a cloak. The two met at the designated spot and walked toward the fields together.

For awhile they simply breathed in the mellow sweetness of spring air about them and watched the men planting the tobacco seeds in the newly cleared ground. Everywhere in the charred remains of autumn burning, the ground was being prepared for the new planting with all available men hoeing the soil and breaking up clods of earth that were packed by winter rains and snows.

In a section of the cleared land, the master supervised the planting of seeds in seedbeds. He apparently trusted no one but himself to the overseeing of the touchy operation. He demanded perfection.

"I have not seen tobacco grow before, so I don't know what it looks like," admitted Charlotte. "When is it ready for harvest?"

"In late summer, I guess."

"How is it taken to market?"

"By flat boats." Maryanne gave very choppy answers. Charlotte realized that the girl was not happy about having her for a temporary governess. No doubt her father had something to do with that. Charlotte decided not to push herself on the girl, for the acceptance would have to be a matter of time.

"Can you play the harp?" asked Charlotte quietly.

"No. I've had no one to teach me."

"I would be happy to teach you if you're interested in learning."

"You?" Maryanne asked with surprise.

"Yes." Charlotte walked along with her eyes straight ahead of her. "My father had both a harpsichord and a harp for the three of us girls to play." She was aware that the girl studied her as they followed the path between the fields.

Suddenly Maryanne looked at her and asked, "Why did you leave your father's house, Miss Grey?"

"Because he and my family died when our house burned." Charlotte continued with her eyes straight ahead, while answering. She still did not look at the girl beside her.

"How awful. Don't you have anyone left?"

"No."

For a little while Maryanne remained silent then she asked, "Where did you go after that?"

"I got a job as a housekeeper."

"And that was the woman who accused you of taking a dish?"

"Yes."

"Did you really do it, Miss Grey?"

"No, I didn't." Charlotte answered softly. "The woman gave me the bowl wrapped in paper and asked me to take it to town and sell it, which I did. When I returned, she told me to put the money in a box by her

122

bed. I told her that I received ten pounds for the dish and I put the money where she told me to.''

''But why would she do that to you?''

''I suspect it was because of her son.''

''Oh? Why was that?''

''He—he was interested in me. I suspect she was not happy about that and wanted me to leave.''

''Why didn't she just tell you to get another job?''

''Her son hired me for one year. We had an agreement.''

Maryanne was quiet once more as they walked slowly alongside the river. Then turning to Charlotte she asked, ''What did her son say when he found out what she did to you?''

''She had me taken away while he was gone. When he returned, I was no longer there.''

''Are you going to go back to England when you leave here and tell him what his mother did to you?''

Charlotte sighed. ''My life is in God's hands, Miss Flaight. I don't know what His plans are for me.''

''If that's so, why did God let this happen to you in the first place?''

''I'm sure He has His reasons. I trust Him to work it out.''

''I wouldn't,'' Maryanne stated defiantly. ''I'd be very angry with the woman—and God.''

''Three years ago I asked the Lord Jesus Christ to come into my heart and take over my life. He did just that. I don't understand all that has happened to me, Miss Flaight, but I have the promise that all things work together for good to them that love God and who are the called according to his purpose.''

''I'd still hate the woman for doing that to me.'' Maryanne lifted her chin upward at a defiant angle.

''Hate is a very strong word. It eats away at one's life and crowds out more worthwhile thoughts. I asked God to help me not to hate his mother.''

The girl sighed. "I would really hate the mother of the man I love if she ever did that to me. I'm very glad that his mother does not live near here."

Charlotte said nothing but she suspected the girl referred to Mr. Blighton. She wondered if the man was aware of this love that Maryanne had for him. She wondered also, how Mr. Flaight would feel about that bit of news if he knew it.

"I would like to learn to play the harp whenever you care to teach me, Miss Grey."

Charlotte nodded then asked, "Can you cook and sew?"

"No."

"I'd be happy to teach you those things, too. If you have a young man in mind, he would be very pleased to know that you are interested in being economical enough to want to learn for his sake."

"Perhaps you're right. Just don't tell my father what I told you."

"I'll not say a word," promised Charlotte. "But he might be happily surprised if you could show him that you know how to be a good housewife. It might help," she smiled, "when the time comes to tell him."

Maryanne proved to be an excellent pupil and eagerly learned all that Charlotte taught her. Each day Maryanne informed her father about her accomplishments. She, like her father, took pride in doing a job well but she was rather impatient and had to be encouraged to finish what she started sometimes.

Charlotte began to receive nods and even an occasional smile from Mr. Flaight. At times, she knew the man studied her, but she pretended not to notice. She didn't want to encourage anything where her employer was concerned.

By the end of May, the trees were arrayed in full green and the second planting of Indian corn was begun in the north sections above the house. From the second story, Charlotte could see the plowers afar off in the field making furrows from one end to the other. Other slaves followed with their supplies of seeds. They dropped them and covered them in a slow, steady rhythm from early morning until dusk. In the river sections and new lands, additional slaves prepared the soil differently with hilling or throwing the dirt into shape by chopping the clods and drawing the earth up, like mole hills, about their inserted feet. This soil would wait for the rains to come before the small tobacco plants could be put in each small hill.

The master frequently walked in the evenings with Mr. Blighton. They talked and studied the sky for signs of rain. Impatiently they waited for the soaking of the fields to do their tobacco planting in the field.

Charlotte knew when the two men did their strolling so she carefully arranged her own walking in the opposite direction or waited until the men returned to the library. She was not eager to cross their paths.

On one particular evening, Charlotte walked toward the river just as the sun was sinking below the strands of red pine to the west. The air was pleasant and warm. No one was in sight, so she ambled along slowly and thought of her former employer and the situation that led to her transport. She felt his presence once more. What would be the situation between them by now if his mother had not had her sent away? she wondered. Would they be married? The thought of being married to Ben Tellison made her happy and she wondered if God would ever work it out that she would be his wife. It seemed so very unlikely now.

Charlotte was so deep in thought that she didn't hear the approach of Mr. Flaight until he stood very near and spoke to her.

"The river is beautiful at sunset, isn't it, Miss Grey?"

Charlotte jumped, shocked that he approached her and spoke to her in such a pleasant manner. "Yes, sir," she answered but she did not turn to him.

He walked ahead of her a few paces and stood very near the water's edge.

"I appreciate what you are doing for Maryanne," he said. "She is learning to sew and cook and play the harp. From what I can see, she's doing a good job."

"Thank you, sir. You can be very proud of her."

For a few moments he said nothing, then he sighed and asked, "Are you sorry that you were brought here, Miss Grey?"

"It's different from England, sir, but no, I'm not really sorry. I trust God to work out my life as He sees fit."

The master stood with his feet apart and his hands folded behind him while he stared down the river. By now the ripples were rose-colored in the light of the setting sun.

"You have said nothing about your former master."

"You never asked me, sir," she whispered.

"Then I am asking you now," he said sharply.

"He was a—a fine man."

"How old was he?"

"Thirty four."

Mr. Flaight studied something along the opposite end of the river for a moment; then he stared out over the water in front of him again. "Is that old to you, Miss Grey?"

"No, sir."

The man thought about her answer a few moments longer then turned abruptly and walked back to the house.

"Good night, Miss Grey," he said over his shoulder.

Charlotte nodded and kept on walking. She couldn't

make much sense out of his conversation but she was surprised that he talked to her that much.

While she turned her face to study the sky, the sun disappeared in a blaze of tinted glory. Then she, too, moved toward the house.

As Charlotte came near the rear door, she saw Maryanne walking in the direction of the steward's office and apartments. Charlotte wondered what the girl was doing. She decided to follow, undetected, and watch. Immoral behavior would not be tolerated by herself or the girl's father.

Maryanne gave a light knock on Mr. Blighton's door. In a few seconds the man opened it and said, "Hello, Maryanne." But he didn't invite her inside.

"I brought you some gingerbread," the girl informed him with a smile. "I hope you like it for I made it special."

"You did?" he commented. "Thank you. It smells delicious."

Maryanne smiled again, turned, and whispered, "Enjoy it. Good night."

Charlotte watched the girl return to the house and go in through the back door. "So, she is attempting to reach his heart through his stomach," she mused. "This should be interesting."

During the night the wind blew strong, rattling the shutters and whistling down the chimneys.

By morning, the rain beat against the earth, strong at first, then steady. It soaked the ground with a thoroughness that caused the master to rouse the slaves and Mr. Blighton to the fields early. For the present, the seed corn lay in the baskets while all hands collected in the tobacco section to draw the hardy young tobacco seedlings from the plant patch. The men, socked through to the skin, proceeded to get the largest of the plants to the new land for transplanting before returning for the smaller ones.

By the time Charlotte made her way to the kitchen, the rain was coming down in steady sheets, soaking the powdery earth into a muddy mass of low lying puddles. The pummeling had no appearance of letting up.

Breakfast was well underway when Charlotte seated herself at the table in the kitchen.

"Da plantin' season done come, praise de Lawd—it done come, Miz Charlotte. But ah's afeard for da men in dis terr'ble rain. Some gets sick fum da soakin'." And she bustled about with an obvious worry about her heavy face.

From the second story window, Charlotte watched the master lead in the activity by taking the plants in baskets while blazing the way to the soil most recently cleared. He dropped plants onto the hills. From there, he proceeded down the rows of mounds while one of the slaves followed, placed the plants in a hole made by his hand, then bolstered it upright with soil for strength.

The rain continued and the work went on until the light no longer afforded them the ability to see the hills of earth piled before them. Not until then, did the men drag themselves weary, worn, and muddy, to their suppers.

The master had John pull off his mud-caked boots and then marched in through the passage with his clothes stuck to his skin and his hair matted to his face.

Charlotte and Maryanne were concerned for the men after such an extended period in the rain. They made a fire in the dining room where the two would eat. When the men came in for supper, Charlotte whispered, "Please sit by the fire to drive off the chill."

"Do you order me about, Miss Grey?" the master barked.

"Yes, sir, I do," she answered.

"Then beware of it," he said sternly. Charlotte smiled, but he sat in the warmest place in spite of her.

"Flaight, you are out to kill us all," said Mr. Blighton when he entered the dining room with a towel about his head and seated himself near the fire. Maryanne moved a footstool near enough for his feet to rest on.

When supper was brought in, John put the meat before the master to carve. "The alternative is starving," said Mr. Flaight acidly.

"Starve, indeed," answered Blighton. "You could easily put the fields out in wheat and corn, make a handsome profit, and be rid of those English leeches who swallow up your profits at such a greedy rate."

The master scowled but would admit nothing. What could he say? He knew it was true. But untangling one's self, especially when you inherit the entanglement from your father as he did, was not as easily done as said. He simply sighed and put a large chunk of meat into his mouth.

Mr. Flaight refused to answer the comment by his steward. The two simply ate their suppers in silence.

Charlotte wondered if the master noticed Maryanne's attentiveness to Mr. Blighton. When he did nothing but stare into his place and scowl, she decided that the man noticed little of anything going on around him unless it dealt with work. *Was he always like this? Was he the same way with his wife when she lived? What kind of a woman was she?* Charlotte wondered. *Did he ever show her any attention?*

One evening after the fields had been planted, Mr. Blighton asked the master's permission to take Maryanne to a party at one of the neighboring estates. Mr. Flaight gave his consent and Maryanne was ecstatically happy. Her eyes had the sparkle of polished jewels.

Charlotte fought a wistful tinge of envy for the

younger girl. She projected her own feelings for just a moment and imagined how she, herself, would feel if it were Ben Tellison making the request that Mr. Blighton had just made. What pleasure she would feel in planning for an evening with him.

"You were right, Miss Grey," Maryanne said excitedly. "My father is noticing how I've changed and how I am now able to cook and sew and play the harp."

"Are you enjoying your accomplishments?"

"Oh, yes. I feel as if I'm doing some good. I'm learning so much and I've now got a purpose to my life—other than spending my time reading."

Charlotte smiled. She was truly pleased for the girl.

On the day of the party, Charlotte volunteered her services as personal maid to help Maryanne prepare for the special event. She brushed the girl's hair until it was glossy then formed lovely fat curls that fell over her bare shoulders and down her back. The lovely pink gown that both Charlotte and Maryanne created had an attractively fitted bodice and billowing skirt that trailed along behind her.

When the blooming Maryanne walked proudly down the central stairway, Mr. Blighton waited for her at the bottom step. The looks in both their eyes told all. They were in love. The young lady appeared much older than her sixteen years of age as she was led to the waiting carriage. Not once did her escort take his adoring eyes from the pretty girl at his side.

Charlotte stood at the open door to watch the carriage rumble along the straight path stretching from the house to the main road beyond. When the coach was out of sight, she stepped down to the walkway following close by the house and across the lawn.

Since it was a pleasant evening, Charlotte ambled down the slope to the river. For a few minutes she watched some chimney swifts making their final little diving rituals before settling down for the night and then she continued on to the water's edge. A pleasantly cooling breeze blew across the ripples. As long as the light continued she walked along the black waters but when it grew too dark to see, Charlotte headed back to the house.

Mr. Flaight was coming across the lawn as she approached the carriage house. He stayed mainly in the shadows so she didn't see the man until he spoke.

"Come and walk with me," he said. "It's such a pleasant night to stroll."

Charlotte was more than a little surprised at the invitation but she reasoned that the man liked company and since Mr. Blighton was gone, he chose her in his place.

She turned and accompanied Mr. Flaight as he walked along. Neither spoke until they approached the river.

"I suspect my daughter has Mr. Blighton on her mind these days."

"It would seem that way, sir."

"Is that why she's learning to cook and sew?"

"I've encouraged her to do it so that she knows how to manage a household. No young woman ought to be helpless."

"True. I'm quite pleased that she has you here with her." At this Charlotte smiled. He certainly had changed from a few weeks ago when he couldn't stand the sight of her.

"You will be here for seven years. At the end of that time, do you plan to go back to England?"

"I don't know, sir. I'm letting the Lord work out that part of my life."

"Is there some reason why you would want to go back? Did you leave a man behind—a man you liked?"

Charlotte chewed on her lower lip for a moment. "There was such a man, yes," she answered softly.

131

"Was he a young man?"

"Fairly young, sir."

"How did he feel about your conviction? Did that make a difference to him?"

"He didn't know about it."

"What do you mean? Why didn't he know?"

"I was accused of stealing and was taken while he was away on business. Before he returned home I was gone. I don't know if he ever learned what happened to me or not. It—it was his mother who did this to me."

"Then he will not want you when he learns that you're a convicted felon. He will take his mother's word for it that you are guilty."

Charlotte was irritated at this remark but she held her temper in check. After all, Mr. Flaight didn't know either her former employer or his mother.

"There is that possibility," she answered evenly, "but I suspect that if he knew the circumstances, he would not accuse me. There was little love in his heart for her."

"So it was your former employer who interested you."

"Yes, it was," Charlotte answered softly.

Mr. Flaight stood with his hands behind his back, legs apart. He studied the sunset beyond the trees then turned his face to glance at the young woman standing near him. For just a moment, his eyes lowered over her entire body.

"It does not matter to me if you are or aren't guilty, Charlotte," he said evenly.

"Thank you, sir, but I assure you I am *not* guilty as accused." She noticed that he used her first name and she had a nagging suspicion he was leading up to something although she didn't exactly know what it was.

When he spoke again he said, "Charlotte, will you marry me?"

She was stunned. "Y—you, sir?" The question he just asked—the proposal—came as a shock. It was obvious that he was kinder to her lately but not once did she ever think that there was anything like this on his mind. It was a while before she collected her senses to rally long enough to answer.

"When I marry, sir," she answered simply, "the man will be God's choice for me."

"Since you were brought here, then I would say that that's your answer."

"No, sir, it is not. There are other things to consider." Charlotte knew that she could never love this man and she must not encourage him to think that she ever would.

"I suppose you are referring to love. That's nonsense. Love is a childish thing and you are more mature than that. I can give you a good home and anything you need."

"Then you are mistaken about me, sir," Charlotte answered firmly. "Love must be a factor in any marriage. If a man or woman is God's choice, love will automatically be there. I do not require a fine home and money to be happy. I can manage on little."

"But you came from a good home. I can tell that."

"Yes, Mr. Flaight, I did. We were happy and there was much love among us."

"Think about what I offer, Charlotte. If you are waiting for that man in England, you wait in vain."

"I don't need to think it over, sir. I cannot marry you; my heart is still with him. It is quite likely that I may never see him again, but that does not stop me from caring deeply for him just the same. But I—I am honored that you would ask me, Mr. Flaight."

"You will change your mind once you've thought it over," he said flatly. "We'll talk about it later—when you've had a chance to consider what I offer you." And with this he said, "Good night, Charlotte."

"Good night, sir."

CHAPTER 9

"MIZ CHARLOTTE," said John one morning at breakfast, "da mastah wish ta see ya in da library."

Charlotte nodded and popped the last of her cornbread into her mouth. She wondered what Mr. Flaight wanted. Surely, she thought as she hurried to the main part of the house, he will not propose again. I'm certain I made it very clear to him that I am not interested.

The master was staring through the window to his green fields beyond when Charlotte came in the room. For awhile he stood silently and said nothing. She waited inside the doorway and studied the man in his fitted black breeches and the homespun shirt that was never tucked in quite as it should be. He was a strong man. Maryanne obviously favored her mother's side of the family for there was little resemblance to her father.

When Mr. Flaight turned he said, "Charlotte, can you manage as both housekeeper and governess for Maryanne?"

"Yes, sir. But Mrs. Langley will be upset—"

"I am not concerned about Mrs. Langley," he bristled. "I keep her simply because my wife had requested it before she died. If she quits tomorrow, that's fine with me. I like what you're doing with my daughter and I want you to continue to teach her household responsibilities even if the woman does come back. As housekeeper, you will be over Mrs. Langley and she will have to abide by your orders."

"I prefer not telling her, sir."

"Then I'll see to it that she understands the situation." He turned, looked at Charlotte a moment, then spoke again. "Maryanne's birthday is in two weeks. Plan something special."

"What is the exact date, sir?"

"June thirtieth."

"Do you want guests invited, Mr. Flaight?" she asked.

"That's up to Maryanne." With this he walked toward Charlotte and stood with his hands behind as he stared directly into her face. "Have you thought about my offer of marriage?"

"Yes, sir," Charlotte replied. "My answer is still the same."

"And I say you are a fool. The man in England will not want you if that's what you are hoping for. Not everyone is willing to overlook a conviction," he snapped.

"But I am not GUILTY, sir." Charlotte returned the look with equal temerity. "If I were, I would be the first to admit such a wrong and I'd do all in my power to make it right. Since I asked the Lord Jesus Christ to live within my heart, I have not had the desire to take what is not mine. He changes lives when He enters into them, sir." she said softly. "He will do the same for you."

"What's wrong with my life, Charlotte?" he demanded. "I work hard and tend to my own affairs."

"But you do not appear happy nor do you give the appearance of having a settled peace in your heart, Mr. Flaight. He can—and will—provide both."

"I don't need sermons. I've not accepted them from the vicar and I won't accept them from you," he breathed unevenly. "I asked you to be my wife. What you think or believe is no concern of mine as long as you keep both to yourself."

"And I cannot marry unless the man is God's choice for me, sir," she said evenly. "That fact will not change."

"We shall see." He sat down at the desk and picked up the quill. "Begin your new duties this morning."

"Yes, sir."

When Maryanne came downstairs she was glowing with the bloom of young love written across her face. "What can I help you with?" she asked. "Papa told me that he was going to make you the housekeeper. Did he talk to you about it?"

"Yes."

"And I'm to help you all I can."

"Then my work will be easy with such excellent help," Charlotte smiled, putting her arm around the girl. "Did Mr. Blighton like your gown last night?"

"Oh, yes," she beamed clasping her hands beneath her chin and turning lightly about. "Don't you think he's divinely handsome, Charlotte?"

"Yes. Very handsome."

When Maryanne moved along beside Charlotte once more she asked, "Was your employer very handsome, too?"

"Yes, but instead of a mop of blond hair, his was dark as chestnuts."

"Like Papa's?" she inquired eagerly, studying Charlotte.

"About the same."

When the two walked outside and moved toward the kitchen, Maryanne took hold of Charlotte's arm. "Stop here a moment," she said. "I need to ask you something."

"Yes?"

"Are—are you interested in Papa?"

"Why do you ask that?" Charlotte queried.

"Because I've seen the way he looks at you. It would seem a little strange to have you for a mother since you are only five years older than I am but—but I wouldn't mind, for you seem more mature than twenty one. I am very fond of you, you know. Would you say yes if he asked you?"

"No, Maryanne, I wouldn't." Charlotte shook her head. "Your father is a hard working man but I can never love anyone as I loved my former employer. I believe he was God's choice for me."

"But what if you never go back to him? You could learn to love Papa. He's a bit harsh at times, but he would be good to you. We could be good friends, you and I, and I would like having you in the family."

"Come, Maryanne, enough of this talk. Your father wants you to learn housekeeping, not work out his choices for a wife."

Mr. Blighton was in the kitchen discussing something with the servants when Charlotte and Maryanne walked in.

"Ah," he said. "I was just talking about you two." He cast a quick wink at Maryanne and then he let his gaze settle on Charlotte. "Everyone has been told about your duties, Miss Grey, and I know you'll have a great helper in Maryanne. The books are in my office and I'll be more than happy to turn them over to you. Your duties will be to plan meals and supervise the sewing, washing, and cleaning. If you'll come with me, I'll show you what to do."

For the second time in less than a year, Charlotte

138

studied the books and manuals of an establishment in preparation for taking over the duties of housekeeper. The difference, of course, lay in two facts; no Madam Tellison would watch her from doorways and no master would make her heart beat quickly whenever he came into view.

The morning of June thirtieth was hot and sticky with just a slight breeze ruffling the leaves of the great elms. Charlotte rose early and hung her alternate blue flowered dress from the limb of a tree by the carriage house so that she'd have something other than her coarse blue gown to wear when the four of them gathered for supper. She had put her hair in papers the night before so she'd look presentable.

After breakfast was cleared away, Maryanne came to Charlotte and asked, "Do you have a special gown to wear tonight? If you don't, you can wear one of mine."

"Won't my flowered one do?"

"Don't you have any others?"

"Well, I—I do have an emerald one but I don't think it would be proper."

"Do let me see it. Please?" Maryanne begged.

"Come along then. It's in my room." Maryanne followed Charlotte to the carriage house and went inside. For a few moments the girl looked around and questioned, "Are you comfortable out here alone? Don't you get afraid at night?"

"No. I ask God to be with me. With Him, I am never afraid."

"Oh, Charlotte," Maryanne said sorrowfully, "you deserve to live somewhere other than this horrible place. If you'd just say yes to Papa, then you could live in the house with us."

"Here is my emerald gown," Charlotte interrupted to change the subject.

"Oh, it's beautiful. Please wear it tonight for my birthday supper. Promise me you will."

"Well, just this once and only because it's special."

Maryanne felt the cloth and then turned to the young woman beside her. "Did your—your former employer have it made for you?"

"Yes."

"And when did you wear it?"

"The last I wore it was for a Christmas banquet."

"Where?"

"At my employer's home."

"Who was there?" Maryanne prodded with interest.

"The captains of Mr. Tellison's ships."

"He's a shipper then?"

"Yes."

"My father ships tobacco. Do you suppose—"

"I don't suppose anything, young lady. Now if you want that special cake tonight, you'd better get to the kitchen and begin making it."

"But you DID promise to wear the emerald dress. Remember?"

"Yes. I'll not forget."

The cook was patient with Maryanne when she directed the making of the special white cake. While it baked, Charlotte took the girl to the dining room and pulled the linens and the porcelains from the chests. As the silverware was being put in place, a rider came galloping to the rear door and knocked. John answered and accepted a letter from the young man who stood there waiting with it in his hand.

"A letter come, Miz Grey," John said.

Charlotte took a quick glance and noticed that it was addressed to Maryanne. "It came on your birthday so it must be special," she said with a smile.

Maryanne ripped open the wax seal and read the contents. "Grandmama and Grandpapa are coming." she stated with enthusiasm. "They'll be here in a week."

"Where do they live?" asked Charlotte arranging the glasses.

"Along the Potomac River. They come by boat once a year to see me."

After Charlotte helped Maryanne dress for supper, she donned her own emerald gown and arranged her hair into curls. At the appointed time, she accompanied the girl down the stairs while both men stared at the two of them descending to the bottom step. Charlotte felt a little foolish but she kept her promise. What Mr. Flaight thought, she couldn't guess but Charlotte refused to glance his way for any reaction from the man. She didn't want him to think that she did any of this for him.

Maryanne kept everyone entertained with stories about Grandpapa and Grandmama Arundel. Mr. Blighton, Charlotte noticed, cast loving glances Maryanne's way throughout the meal. She felt certain that there would be a wedding at Flaight Plantation some time in the not too distant future.

Charlotte sighed under her breath. How she wished that she, too, were with the man she loved.

After the cake was eaten, Mr. Blighton took Maryanne's arm, and Mr. Flaight put his hand into Charlotte's arm with a soft, "you look very pretty tonight, Miss Grey. Why haven't you worn that dress before?"

"It's hardly appropriate for my duties so far, sir," she said with a droll twist of her mouth. "Scrubbing is hardly the occupation for satin gowns."

"Then I suggest we find more occasions for you to wear it." Charlotte didn't agree but she said no more. This was a special night and she'd not spoil it with arguing.

Maryanne entertained her birthday guests with her first harp concert. She had mastered two pieces before she rose and looked at the older girl in emerald.

"Charlotte," she said with a smile, "please play a few numbers for us and show us how this lovely instrument OUGHT TO sound."

"You did very well, Maryanne, and I don't want to take from your special night."

"Nonsense." interrupted Mr. Flaight. "Do as she asks."

Charlotte seated herself at the instrument and strummed through the first piece. Then as she was beginning her second, a tall, thin figure appeared at the doorway and assessed the situation with anger written across her twisted face.

"What is this contemptible person doing in your drawing room, Mr. Flaight," she hissed, "and in the company of your daughter?"

"Hold your tongue, Langley!" spat the master. With this he rose angrily and forcefully accompanied the woman into another room with a firm closing of a door behind them.

Charlotte felt the heat of humiliation rise to her neck and face. In her eyes salt drops gathered. Was there no end to the degradation she had to endure? She began to rise from her seat, but Maryanne and Mr. Blighton both demanded that she continue until the piece was finished.

"Don't pay any heed to the woman," insisted Mr. Blighton firmly. "She spoke out of turn—and without basis. Please continue. It is Maryanne's birthday and I won't have it spoiled."

So, for Maryanne's sake, Charlotte continued. By now, however, it was no longer a pleasure—it was a forced performance. Her breath came in tight little spurts and the restrictive lodging in her throat was the size of a turnip. "Oh, Lord," she said under her breath, "in some way—somehow—deliver me from all this wretched debasement."

The following day Charlotte informed the servants

of the pending visit of the Arundels. Together they pulled linens from drawers and chests, to air, and caused such a bustle about the house with cleaning, scrubbing, dusting, and extra baking, that it would have put any fighting regiment to shame. Maryanne dived into the preparations in spite of loud protest from Mrs. Langley.

Prior to the visit, Mr. Flaight was more irritable and short tempered than usual and Charlotte suspected that he loathed the coming visit of his in-laws. On several occasions she heard loud, angry words between the master and Mrs. Langley so she kept out of the way of both.

"Why doesn't he just pension the woman?" Charlotte asked herself. "It would be simpler than fighting, I should think."

By late afternoon of the following week, the grandparents arrived by boat and the servants assisted them from the vessel to the house—along with a little maid who reminded Charlotte of a mouse.

John announced their arrival to the master then proceeded to help take their baggage to the assigned room on the second floor.

Maryanne could no longer restrain herself. She came down the stairway with Mrs Langley following—out of breath—by the time they reached the last step.

"Grandpapa and Grandmama!" she cried while the two engulfed her with a great display of affectionate hugs and kisses, plying the same on Mrs. Langley.

Charlotte stayed well out of the way until Mr. Flaight approached and said, "Mr. and Mrs. Arundel, this is my housekeeper, Miss Grey. She will take you to your room and see that everything is comfortable." And then turning to John, he ordered, "Have tea ready in half an hour."

The master showed no emotion and disappeared as

quickly as he could back to his office. A hush came over the group for just an instant when he withdrew so hastily. Mrs. Langley scowled angrily then accompanied the group to the second story, staying close to Mrs. Arundel during the entire procedure.

Charlotte followed the procession and studied the woman in front of her. She was fiftyish, pretty—but unsmiling—with light hair and blue eyes. Her figure was slender in her black taffeta and she was obviously a lady of very proper breeding. Mrs. Arundel held her head high as she climbed the stairs. She strode as a queen to her coronation while her dress trailed behind, brushing and rustling on the steps as she walked upward.

When the procession entered the appointed room, Charlotte pulled back the curtains to allow the room the full benefits of light.

"Bring me some warm water in a basin," Mrs. Arundel demanded of the housekeeper as her mousey little maid assisted her in removing her hat. Charlotte did not cower under the woman's stern look and biting tongue. She simply bit her lip and answered calmly, "I'll have it sent up, Madam." She would not give the woman the pleasure of making her angry.

Mr. Arundel was standing nearby whistling softly under his breath but saying nothing. He was a jovial man with bright eyes, pink cheeks, double chin, and a stomach that was over sized for his sparse height.

Charlotte went to the kitchen and found Annie preparing the tea. The woman sidled over to her and whispered, "Dat lady gots a bitin' tongue, Miz Charlotte. Don' you fret none wi' da likes a her."

"Thanks, Annie," Charlotte whispered back. "I'll keep that in mind." She knew Mrs. Arundel would be difficult—about everything.

By evening Maryanne was dressed and in high spirits for a performance on the harp. The master arranged for Charlotte to be in the drawing room when they entered from supper and he found her waiting as arranged.

Grandpapa accompanied Maryanne from the dining room to the drawing room followed by Mrs. Arundel, the master, Mrs. Langley, and Mr. Blighton.

Charlotte was already seated in a back corner of the room where she had placed her mending, beforehand, near a candlestand.

Maryanne seated herself at the harp and plucked the tunes that were practiced endlessly during the previous weeks. When she completed her piece, the girl walked over to sit by Mr. Blighton.

"Where did you learn to play the harp?" Mrs. Arundel asked in surprise when Maryanne smiled at her grandparents.

"From Miss Grey," the girl answered simply.

"Miss Grey?" asked her grandmother in a shocked voice. "I thought she was a housekeeper."

"Of late, yes," Mrs. Langley threw in.

"What do you mean?"

"She was a scrub woman before I left."

"Is this true? Just where did you find her, Flaight?" asked Mrs. Arundel turning her head to look at her son-in-law.

"From England," the master answered flatly.

"But how?" She waited a moment for an answer and when he hesitated she prodded, "Tell me."

"From a ship, of course. She didn't walk."

"One of the servant ships?" Here Mr. Flaight attempted to change the subject by saying, "Would you care for tea?" and he stood to his feet and walked to the doorway.

"Flaight, why aren't you answering me?" demanded the woman angrily.

"Because, Madam, it really makes no difference what she came on, does it? She is here."

At this Mrs. Arundel looked at the governess and the woman blurted out triumphantly, "A convict ship, Mrs. Arundel."

"What are you saying?" The lady bolted upright in her chair and stared first at the governess and then at the master. "Is this true? This woman is a CONVICT?"

Mr. Flaight didn't answer but looked straight ahead of him.

"Flaight," hissed the woman through her teeth.

He still refused to answer.

"Do you mean to tell me that you left Maryanne in that woman's care for two months while her governess was away?"

"I do. And as you can see, she is well; she survived."

"How dare you?" she said with venom in her voice. "She is my daughter's child." With this, Mrs. Arundel rose in anger.

"And mine, madam." The master answered matching her seething anger and looking into her face as he spoke.

Charlotte again felt deep shame and humiliation at being the subject of discussion in so degrading a manner. She was grateful when Mr. Flaight's voice said, "Miss Grey, you may be excused." She rose and without looking at the two women, she left as quickly as she could.

For the next few days Charlotte saw little of the governess, but she saw Mrs. Arundel often. The woman would call her continually to do small menial tasks for her—tasks that were the little maid's duty to perform. But Charlotte did them all with courtesy and dignity, for Mr. Flaight's sake, for she would not give the woman the pleasure of stirring her anger.

Mr. Arundel spent his days in entertaining Maryanne and casting sly, earthy glances at the housekeeper when he wasn't following the master about the plantation inspecting the crops.

One morning Mrs. Arundel cornered Mr. Flaight in the drawing room. Charlotte worked across the hall and could not help but hear the woman's unpleasant voice drifting in from the partially closed doorway.

"Mr. Flaight, I am concerned that my granddaughter is with this wicked base creature that you have here."

"What vile things did you observe in Maryanne that you didn't see a year ago?"

"Do be serious!" she demanded in anger.

"Oh, I have never been more serious in my life."

"Then I have a proposition to put to you, sir."

If Mr. Flaight replied, Charlotte did not hear it for the lady continued on with her speaking.

"You can sell this creature for the price you paid for her?"

"I could, yes." A moment passed then he added, "But I won't."

"And why not?"

"If I wanted to do that, why do you think she came here in the first place?"

"You seem to have plenty of servants without her," the woman commented. "Sell her to me."

"Why? So you can make her work for you and let your maid sit idle? You seem to enjoy making my housekeeper do your tasks for you. Is that what your housekeeper does in your house?"

"She is beneath anything that I have in my house, Flaight."

"But not in mine. On the contrary, she is the best."

"How dare you place her in a position above Mrs. Langley—the governess who was her whole life with my daughter? She glared with a hateful lift to her chin while she studied the man she talked with. "Or is it that this girl is pretty and you have something else in

147

mind, sir? She perhaps is good to you, eh? You can easily slip out to that pen in the carriage house, can't you?'' she screamed.

"Madam, hold that tongue in your head or I will ask you to leave my house!" he bellowed.

"If I do, it will be with Maryanne accompanying me."

"You seem to forget, madam, that I have the say about Maryanne. If you are intent on taking someone with you, take Langley. You're WELCOME to her!"

"And leave that poor child to that convict? Never."

"Then leave things as they are."

Mrs. Arundel tried a fresh approach to getting what she wanted by adding sweetly, "You surely know how much Maryanne loves her grandparents. Why can't we have her? After all, you are so busy with the company you seldom have time for her."

"Because she is getting married."

"Married?" The woman was audibly stunned. "To whom? And why wasn't I told?"

"That will be announced in time, but I shall not tell you until the arrangements are made."

"Where could she possibly meet a man of breeding here in this wilderness?" she demanded.

"You will find out," he answered curtly.

"So," Charlotte mused. "Maryanne will get her wish for a husband after all. What did Mr. Blighton say to him—and when?" Charlotte was happy for the girl and hoped Maryanne would make a good wife for the young steward. *How wonderful to marry the man you love*, she thought wistfully.

After a week, Mrs. Langley spoke to Charlotte while the breakfast remains were being cleared from the dining room. "Mrs. Arundel has brought me some lovely gifts and I don't want them handled when you dust the tops of the chests and tables. Do you understand?"

"Mrs. Langley, I shall not touch them at all," Charlotte said softly, walking away from the woman and into the hallway.

For a day or two the house and occupants seemed settled and somewhat agreeable. Mrs. Arundel's maid spoke very little to any of the servants at the house except to inform them that, "The Arundel house is much larger and finer."

"It certainly is," agreed Mrs. Langley, overhearing the maid. "I certainly regretted having to leave the place, and the town, for there were so many interesting things to do there. Not like this country." She sighed a deep sigh. "If only Mrs. Flaight was still alive, she would liven it up here. This is no place for Maryanne. She'll never find a decent husband here."

While Charlotte attended to putting the supper dishes away, Mrs. Langley came to the drawing room where the master and Mr. Blighton were talking.

"Mr. Flaight—it's missing!" the woman said angrily.

"What the devil are you talking about?" he snapped.

"The porcelain jewel case that Mrs. Arundel brought me. It's gone from my room."

"So? Look for it."

"I already have. I'm sure it's that convict you have here in your house."

"You've just misplaced it," said the master flatly.

"I have not!" she cried. "I searched the entire room, moved furniture, went through drawers, and I tell you, sir, it's not there."

Mr. Flaight reluctantly sent John for his housekeeper and when she entered the room, the two women looked as if they would eat her limb by limb.

"Miss Grey, did you see my new porcelain jewel case on the table when you dusted?"

Charlotte stared at the woman. "Yes, madam. I

did." Charlotte answered softly. "It was on your table yesterday."

"And did you move it?"

"No, I did not. I touched nothing on your table." Charlotte looked directly into the woman's eyes for she suspected trickery of some sort.

"Then it's strange that I cannot find it."

"I shall be happy to help you look."

"It is," said the woman angrily, "GONE!"

"I'm sorry. If I can help, I will." Charlotte refused to leave their presence and continued to watch their faces.

"Flaight, search her apartment," demanded Mrs. Arundel.

"Miss Grey wouldn't take it, Grandmama," said Maryanne from the doorway where she had been listening to the conversation.

"She would—and did. No one ELSE would."

"You are excused, Miss Grey," said the master.

Charlotte went directly to the kitchen but she was uneasy about the matter. All the horrors of the last day at Tellison Hall came back to her as a flood—a sickening, overpowering wave. "Work it out, Lord," she whispered, "Please work this thing out."

That evening as she was checking on the supplies for the next day, Charlotte again overhead Mrs. Arundel with the master.

"It's a horrible thing to allow that woman the full use of this house as you do. Have you investigated to see if she has stolen other articles of value? Is your silver all accounted for?"

"Madam, I don't care about that jewel case or anything else around here, and I want you out of this house in the morning!"

"Then we WILL leave in the morning!" And she flew out in a rage.

At daybreak, Mrs. Arundel's flustered maid was

hurrying about packing portmanteaus while John carried the bulging cases to the first story for the servants to put on the boat.

The master was standing by the door talking to Mr. Arundel. The man's wife came down the stairway followed by Mrs. Langley. She adjusted her bonnet while her maid brought one last case, but as the girl walked toward her mistress, she stumbled and the contents of the case spread about the floor with an accompanying crash against the leg of one of the tables.

Everyone turned and as each did so, Maryanne saw something on the floor beneath the table and cried out. "Look, Grandmama, here is the porcelain jewel case that was missing. I knew Miss Grey wouldn't take it." And she innocently picked up the pieces of it and handed them to her Grandmama.

The onlookers stood in dumb silence—awkward and embarrassed. Mrs. Arundel held her head high and declared, "I can't imagine how it got in my case."

"Can't you?" the master said raising his face and staring in anger.

At this, Mrs. Arundel swung around to the doorway. "Pick up my things," she snapped at her awkward maid and walked on toward the boat. Mr. Arundel followed his wife silently while the flustered maid clamored about picking up her mistress' things in an agony of shame and terror.

Mrs. Langley retreated into a silent exit but Mr. Flaight turned and demanded, "What have you to say about this?"

The woman refused to make any comment and marched stiffly up the stairs to her room.

Charlotte breathed a sigh of relief. "Thank you, Lord," she whispered under her breath. "I couldn't survive without You."

CHAPTER 10

THE JULY MORNING WAS WARM and humid. Charlotte took her mending and a small bench onto the front lawn so she could work under the shade of the tulip tree and enjoy the fresh river breezes. For a few minutes she watched vessels sailing with the currents, carrying loads destined for foreign ships anchored in the coastal water at the seaport.

Cardinals, robins, and swallows pecked and chirped their busy hours away by tending to little ones hidden about in the boxwood and ivy. Charlotte's mind, however, was not centered on any of these things. It was on the master. While her fingers worked, she thought about her life and the offer to be mistress of Flaight Plantation. It was a lovely estate and she could be happy here, if she were married to Ben Tellison. She knew that she could never be happy married to Mr. Flaight. She sighed. Seven years was a long time to wait.

While Charlotte worked, she heard John's shuffling steps moving across the lawn toward her.

"A horseman is here, Miz Grey."

She arose immediately from her work and went to find the fellow. Two letters were handed to her; one for Mrs. Langley and the other, her heart freezing at the sight of it, was from Tellison Shipping Co. in Lynnhampton. It was addressed to Mr. Flaight. For a moment Charlotte completely forgot all courtesy. When she looked up, and her voice returned to her once again, she saw the rider galloping away down the lane.

"Thank you, sir!" she cried after him. "Thank you!"

The boy waved and continued back to the village.

Charlotte turned the letter for the governess over in her hand and discovered that it was sealed in black. "John, please take this to Mrs. Langley." She handed it to him but her eyes were already searching the envelope that she held in her other hand.

"Yas'm." He resumed his shuffling gait across the grass and into the house.

For awhile Charlotte stood and held the letter from Tellison Shipping. She swallowed the lump of excitement that formed in her throat, realizing that this message came from the one man who meant more to her than anyone in the whole world. Perhaps he even held it in his hand before he ordered it placed on one of his ships destined for the Virginia seaport.

"What is this letter about?" she whispered. Charlotte chewed on her lower lip while she speculated. Would she dare write Mr. Tellison a letter and tell him of her whereabouts? Just as quickly as the thought popped into her head, she dispelled the notion. What if he didn't believe that she was innocent of her conviction? No, she could never contact him. It would be better to wonder than to be told outright that he could not accept her explanation. Again she sighed. What did the future possibly hold for her?

"Oh, Lord," she breathed softly, "work out your will for my life."

Charlotte started slowly, thoughtfully, back to the house to place Mr. Flaight's letter on his desk. She knew the contents of Mrs. Langley's letter was not good news and she wanted to be available if the woman desired a sympathetic ear. She went into the house as Maryanne came down the stairway to find her.

"Mrs. Langley is crying, Miss Grey. It's the letter. No doubt her sister passed away."

"Yes, I'm sure it's that," Charlotte said.

Within minutes, Mrs. Langley came down the steps and announced simply, "I must leave."

Immediately Charlotte went to her to offer any condolence that she might accept. "I'm sorry to hear it, Mrs. Langley." But when Charlotte put her hand forward to place it on the woman's arm, Mrs. Langley drew back as if a viper had approached her.

"I'll help if I can," Charlotte said ignoring the reaction.

"My sister has died and I will need to leave immediately. She was my only sister." The woman remained tall and straight while she wept silently.

If she would have permitted it, Charlotte would have gathered the woman in her arms and held her close to comfort and cry with her in her sorrow, but Mrs. Langley wanted none of it. Immediately Charlotte was reminded of Jesus' words when he looked at the people of Israel and wanted to gather them to him as a hen would chicks, but they rejected him, also. She knew his pain must have been even harder to bear.

"I, too, have felt pain for family," Charlotte whispered, "but the Lord Jesus will help you bear if it you ask Him."

The woman disregarded the remark entirely and said simply, "Inform the master for me."

154

Charlotte nodded but said no more. Mrs. Langley turned abruptly and left the two of them standing in the passage to watch helplessly while she moved toward her room. Charlotte put her arm around Maryanne's shoulder and walked out to the lawn. "Pain touches all of us some time or other but we don't need to bear it alone."

When the master and Mr. Blighton returned from the fields, Maryanne informed them of Mrs. Langley's forthcoming departure.

For just an instant Charlotte thought she detected a thin smile on the master's lips, but he turned so suddenly that she couldn't be entirely certain. "Tell her I want to see her before she leaves."

"Yes, sir," Charlotte said.

After the noon meal, Mrs. Langley appeared before the master in the library. Charlotte was putting the dining room in order after the dishes were removed from the table and could not help overhearing them speak.

"Mrs. Langley, I understand you are leaving."

"Not permanently," she said. "I will be back for I wouldn't want Miss Maryanne to be in the hands of . . . be without a governess."

The master was silent for a moment. "I will pension you immediately. Maryanne will be getting married soon and you will not be needed. You can live in the village and be independent."

"Never! I promised your dear wife I would stay with Maryanne until she married." With this, she flew from the room and disappeared through the entrance while John followed and placed her bag in the carriage.

Maryanne helped Charlotte with her duties and then the two went for a walk toward the fields.

A few cotton clouds floated lazily in the clear sky on their journeys from here to there. Charlotte and

Maryanne followed the road outside the criss-cross worm fence. When they came to the fields, they watched the slaves wield their hoes, continually working the ground around the hills of tobacco and between the rows. It was a backbreaking job for they straightened from time to time to relieve the stiffness of remaining too long in one position. The men wore neither shoes nor stockings but worked in white canvas pants to the knees, with their backs exposed to the heat of the sun.

In the days that followed, Charlotte wondered about the letter that came for the master marked, Tellison Shipping. He said nothing nor had it changed his mood since its arrival. She wondered what it could signify. Why would he get a letter from Mr. Tellison? Charlotte tried unsuccessfully to form, in her mind, a logical reason for its being in the master's possession but when she couldn't, she endeavored to dismiss it from her mind.

One afternoon the steward came in from the fields while the master was eating a late diner. "Sir, we have found the horn worm in the old field."

Mr. Flaight immediately rose and slammed his hat on his head. "How many did you find?" he asked.

"Several."

At this news the master was visibly shaken and demanded to know the exact spot in which they were discovered.

"All in the old ground but we haven't looked further."

Maryanne and Charlotte stood frozen by the back entrance as the men rushed past. Both guessed that the things the men discussed were something to be dreaded.

'This tobacco," Charlotte commented, "is it really worth the agony it causes? Surely wheat, corn, or sugar beets would not be the heartache that this crop causes."

156

"Mr. Blighton doesn't think it is," said Maryanne. "He doesn't plan to grow it on his land."

"Is his property near here?" asked Charlotte.

"About five miles away to the north. It is just a small property for he is his father's second son. The large estate was left to his older brother. But we'll manage," said Maryanne confidently. "Now that I can cook and sew, we will get along fine."

"When do you plan to marry?"

"As soon as harvest is over in September. I want you at my wedding, Charlotte, for you're the best friend I've ever had."

"I will if I can," answered Charlotte. But after she gave Maryanne her answer, she wondered what made her reply that way.

For days the men carefully inspected every plant for the dreaded green horned worms and after locating them pulled the horrible things from the leaves to be killed.

As soon as breakfast was over in the morning, every available hand was ordered to the fields to inspect the crop.

At night the men crawled from the fields in a state of utter exhaustion, weary in muscle and spirit.

"Never saw so many as this year," said the master. "They're everywhere."

"I think, sir," said the steward, "we'll have to make continuous checks for fresh signs." As soon as supper was over, the men went to their beds only to wake the following day with the job yet undone before them.

Charlotte was careful to keep Maryanne and herself out of their way.

During the morning, gray clouds appeared in the sky—gradually at first—and then with increased concentration until the sun was blotted from the sky and a few droplets of water fell gently on the window panes.

By noon, the drops had become a steady rain that penetrated the earth to the root and sent small rivers of water running jagged and erratic down the panes.

Charlotte truly hoped, for the men's sakes, that the rain would let up somewhat but it was not the case. The worming went on.

All day the gray sky poured its heavy soaking. It continued into the evening until the men dragged themselves, filthy, with their clothes sticking to their skins, into supper. Charlotte and Maryanne had fires going in the fireplaces so the master and Mr. Blighton could toast their chilled, rain-soaked bodies at the fire before they ate.

The night brought no relief from the deluge. Charlotte didn't attempt to get to her apartment in the carriage house, but instead took a blanket and settled herself comfortably on a sofa in the library while the rain pelted the panes and lulled her into a fitful dozing. From time to time she awoke and listened. When the drenching continued, she slipped to her knees by the sofa. "Oh, God," she whispered, "let the rain stop for I fear for the health of the men and the safety of the crops. Our people need to be fed and clothed. Even now they may be suffering from exposure and illness." She pictured the slaves in their drafty quarters with rain pummeling the roofs and perhaps leaking through to the floors.

How long she stayed on her knees she couldn't remember. When Charlotte opened her eyes again, a hushed stillness was in the room and she realized that an eerie light showed through the window beyond her.

"The moon!" she cried. "The rain has stopped!" With a heart full of gratitude, she ran to the window to look out upon the cool bathed earth lying in ghostlike whiteness about her.

Mrs. Langley returned after one week's absence and continued to object to Maryanne's learning household duties. The woman complained that it was not proper training for a young lady of breeding. But in spite of objections, Maryanne continued to help Charlotte with the work.

During the second week in August, Charlotte and Maryanne were making preserves when a letter arrived addressed to Charlotte. She was stunned. Who could possibly be writing to her? Her fingers were visibly shaking in her haste to pry off the seal and pull the paper apart to read the words that had been written. When her heart calmed and she was able to gain control of her senses and limbs once more, she read the bold scrawl—the hand that she knew so well. It contained the familiar flourishes as the letter she already had safely hidden in her bosom.

With lips that were drained of all color, she read:

"Dear Charlotte,

I learned from the lieutenant of the JUSTICE what happened to you. I will be at the seaport on one of my ships in September for the banquet aboard ship. Mr. Flaight knows about it and has been invited. I must see you.

Ben Tellison"

Charlotte closed the letter and leaned against the wall for support.

Maryanne studied her carefully and saw the white face. "What is it?" she asked hurrying to her side. "Bad news?"

"It—it's from my former employer," she whispered. "He wants to meet me at the seaport in September, at the planters' banquet."

"Oh, Charlotte, what do you suppose he will say to you?"

159

"I—I don't know, Maryanne."

One thing that Charlotte DID know was that Lieutenant Drummond made his way back to England—and on a Tellison ship. He had talked to Ben Tellison and told him the story that she had related to him.

But what about the letter? Her feelings concerning the writer had not changed in all these months. His may have changed drastically. Charlotte carefully folded the letter and placed it in her bosom with the other one.

"This explains the letter your father got from my former employer," she said. "It was an invitation to a banquet aboard ship. No doubt all the planters from the area, who send him hogsheads of tobacco, were invited to attend." She wondered if Mr. Flaight would go and if she would be able to accompany him.

"Yes, that's what the letter was about. I went with Papa last year for he had no one else to take. But this year, I was hoping he could take you." Maryanne was silent for a few moments then she added softly, "Your prayers have been answered, Charlotte, and the man you love is coming for you."

"I don't know what he will say to me. That remains to be seen."

Charlotte wondered, too, what she would say to Mr. Tellison and what he would say to her. It had been so long. Would he tell her what it was that he planned to say to her the evening he returned from his journey? Exactly what would it have been? Charlotte's mind was in a spin and she honestly wondered if she would be able to survive until the end of September. That was still six weeks away.

How will I bear it until then? she wondered. *Will he condemn me?*

The master sent for Charlotte to come to him in the library one evening after an especially trying day in the tobacco-drying barns. It had been a day spent struggling with fires, and temperatures, and drafts until he despaired of the whole operation of heating as a lesson in utter futility against human endurance.

He stood at the window with his back to her. The sunset threw long shadows behind him while he stood defiant, straight, and strong staring into its fiery evening softness. His body was lean and hard from strong physical labors. His hair fell thick and brown to the center of his back, held in control by a black ribbon that drooped pitifully from months of excessive use. His powerful arms arched and rested on browned hands that gripped hips made slender by hours of bending in the fields.

Charlotte remained silent until he turned, in his own time, to find her at his hearth and waiting his bidding.

"Charlotte," he said moving toward where she stood. "Each autumn the shipper who carries my tobacco to England has a banquet aboard his ship. It's for the planters, like myself, who send hogsheads to these English merchants."

At this announcement, the girl's heart pounded within her breast for she knew it was Mr. Tellison whom he would meet aboard that vessel. Charlotte awaited his words with great anxiety on her part.

The master stood before her with legs apart and hands behind him, looking down at the floor and displaying a rather nervous manner before he spoke to her.

"Would you like a new gown—a silk one—something pretty perhaps? Young women like to appear well dressed. You will accompany me to that supper. It will be at the end of September, in about three weeks. I will take you to the village in the morning and you can choose a cloth. The choice may not be so

161

great but you can look." He glanced at the girl for an answer.

"I am honored that you ask me but I, also, got a letter requesting me to meet my former employer on board that ship."

For a few minutes Mr. Flaight stared at the girl standing before him. "And what did he tell you about your conviction?"

"He didn't say anything except to ask me to meet him. The letter was—was rather impersonal."

"Then don't expect that he will be in a forgiving mood when you walk on board."

"That, sir, remains to be seen." Charlotte said softly. If she were honest with herself, she would have to admit that she harbored a few doubts herself. Then with a lift of her chin, she said, "Whatever answer the Lord has for me, I will accept it. He will give me grace to bear it, if it is a rejection."

"Then you can be sure you'll need it. Don't forget my offer for it still stands."

"Thank you, sir."

"We'll go to the village in the morning."

"That's not necessary, Mr. Flaight, for my emerald dress has only been worn twice and it will do."

"Nonsense. Be ready at nine o'clock."

When Charlotte left the library she saw Mrs. Langley glaring at her through fiery eyes that glowed with renewed hatred. Charlotte's flesh crawled at the memory of those vicious eyes upon her and it wasn't until she crossed the walkway to the kitchen beyond—through the cleansing summer breezes—that she rid herself of the woman's deep loathing for her.

The following morning dawned warm and red-streaked with a silent breeze barely moving the late summer green on the trees. Charlotte drew water for an early bath before she donned her flowered dress in anticipation of the promised venture into the village.

After she had adjusted her gown and given a final touch to her hair, Charlotte went to the kitchen for breakfast.

"Lawsa me, Miz Grey. Yo got somethin' special t' do t' day, sho nuff."

Charlotte smiled. "Yes, the master is taking me to the village."

"He needs cheerin', dat man does. Dat Miz Langlay, she's a wearin' t' da mastah."

"Why should that be, Annie?" Charlotte asked.

"Don' know. I sho don'." Annie popped a piece of hot apple into her mouth and they ate in silence. Perhaps the reason was simply that Mrs. Langley was carrying out a promise to Mrs. Flaight on her deathbed—the promise that she would stay with Maryanne until the girl got married. It was apparent that Mr. Flaight was not at all pleased about that promise.

Charlotte went to the second story to close the curtains to make sure that all was in order before she proceeded on to the top of the stairs. Looking below, she saw Mr. Flaight waiting for her. She placed one foot on the top step and began descending. He continued to watch her until Mrs. Langley suddenly appeared behind him in the passage below. The woman looked first at the master and then at Charlotte before she cried out to him.

"So! You have the nerve to wait for that girl do you—a girl young enough to be your daughter? What would your wife say? Hm? What would Meribel say if she knew this convict made Maryanne do housework?" She screamed louder and louder. "Have you no shame? Tell me! What— —" Mrs. Langley suddenly choked and fell, clutching her chest in an agony of pain. She stumbled first to her knees, then unsteadily collapsed onto one arm, and finally to the floor.

Charlotte was too stunned to move. She stood frozen, gripping the railing with both hands to steady herself while the master stared at the stricken woman on the floor. His mouth was a thin, taut line as he moved toward her. From behind him, Mr. Blighton rushed to where Mrs. Langley lay crumpled and unconscious on the floor.

Mr. Flaight felt the woman's pulse and knelt beside her to check for signs of breathing. "She's dead." His announcement was simple and quiet. He rose and looked at his steward. "Tell the carpenter what to do. I'll take her to her room." With this, the master knelt again, picked up the limp body of the governess, and carried it to her room above. Charlotte stood as a dumb beast, staring at the man as if this whole thing were a horrible dream.

"Well, it's over," said Mr. Blighton when he walked up the steps to accompany her to the bottom of the steps. "It had to be—sooner or later. One cannot hate to such a degree and not be affected by it." When he reached the last step, the steward turned and spoke. "I must find the carpenter and give him the message." He left through the rear passage to carry out the master's orders.

In a matter of minutes, Mr. Flaight returned to the lower hallway. "We'll go to the village another day," he said stiffly.

"Of course," Charlotte whispered.

By late afternoon, a cool shower had driven a few of the prematurely crimson leaves from the trees and matted the taller grasses flat against the ground.

The small procession consisting of the master, Mr. Blighton, Maryanne, and Charlotte made their way through the sodden grass with the wooden coffin. They guided the horse-pulled cart to a small plot where several graves nestled among the weeds of a fenced enclosure.

"She loved my wife so she would have wanted to be buried beside her," Mr. Flaight stated flatly and without any emotion whatsoever.

Charlotte was asked to read the appropriate words from a large Bible. She felt cold and sickened by the fact that the woman lying in the wooden coffin before her left nothing but hate behind her. Not once did she try to make amends for her lies or ask forgiveness. Charlotte could only hope that in her last seconds of life, she called upon God to cleanse her heart of the great weight of sin. All Charlotte could do was read the scriptures that would speak to the living gathered around her—words of exhortation to give their lives to Christ before it was too late and they, too, would have no further opportunity to make their lives right before God. "Seek and ye shall find . . . " she continued reading in a straightforward voice—confident and unwavering.

A couple of the slaves had dug the hole and helped the man lay Mrs. Langley into the earth. The clods of dirt were replaced around the coffin and then the group, without speaking, made its way back to the house.

The master's mouth remained a hard, taut, unyielding line and he shed no tears for Mrs. Langley. No doubt the woman's departure was a great relief lifted from his shoulders.

Annie had hot soup waiting for their supper. After the meal was eaten, Charlotte walked slowly to her apartment in the carriage house.

"What a futile thing hate is," she whispered in the growing darkness, "and how tragic it is to be consumed by the sin, leaving nothing behind but the memory of a life that consisted of ashes."

CHAPTER 11

CHARLOTTE WAS GLAD that she had the wedding to help the time go faster during the three weeks before the planters' banquet. She helped Maryanne sew the lovely white satin that was bought in Williamsburg. Once the final stitches were completed, the gown would be gloriously beautiful and Maryanne would make a stunning bride for James Blighton on their wedding day.

Charlotte was pleased that Maryanne was learning to be an excellent housekeeper. She could sew the tiniest of fine stitches and her cooking was improving each day. She used every opportunity to make recipes that pleased both her betrothed and her papa as well.

"What will your father do when he no longer has James to help him on the estate?" asked Charlotte pulling off more thread to stitch the bodice together.

"Papa's trying to persuade him to stay here and build a house on a section of the plantation."

"How does James feel about that?"

"He wants to manage on his own and show Papa

that he is able to support me. James has a small independent income but we'll have to budget very carefully if we are to live on the amount," answered Maryanne. "I think, though, that much will depend on you." The statement was added quietly and with a quick glance toward the housekeeper while she drew the needle in and out of the cloth.

"Me?" asked a shocked Charlotte, glancing at the girl while the needle remained immobile in mid air.

"Yes, Charlotte. You see, if you would marry Papa, he would have someone to live with him, make him happy, and he wouldn't miss me so much. This concerns both James and me and it will make a difference in our plans."

Charlotte thought about Maryanne's statement. She wondered if the steward had this plan in mind when he purchased her from the ship. She chewed on her lower lip in thoughtful silence before she answered. "Maryanne, I can make no promises about marriage. If Ben wants me to be his wife, and his life is right before God, I will accept. My sentiments for him are the same as those you have for James. The only way that I would feel differently is if God would change that. You do understand that, don't you, Maryanne?" she asked gently, pleadingly.

"Yes, I guess I do. It's just that it seems such a perfect answer to our problems," she said quietly, with a touch of apology in the tone of her voice.

"Then pray about it, Maryanne, and God will work it out. He will send a woman for your father to marry—a woman he can truly love."

"You pray about everything, don't you, Charlotte?" asked the girl, stopping a few moments from her stitching to study the housekeeper sitting next to her.

"Yes. That way you can be sure the outcome will always be right," Charlotte responded.

"And does your Ben pray about things, too?"

"Yes. I'm sure he does, for in his note to me before I left, he said he was going to London to make something right in his life. He asked God to forgive him."

"Did he do something terribly bad?"

"He didn't say, but the scriptures tell us we have all sinned and that small sins are as evil as large sins in God's sight. Everyone must be forgiven. When we ask Christ to forgive us and come into our lives, he cleanses us from all unrighteousness and gives us peace plus eternal life."

It was extremely sultry for September. The stifling humidity plus Charlotte's restless thoughts mixed with the steady night sounds beyond her window—an owl calling from an ash near the river, the crickets in the ivy beds.

When sleep would not come, she rose and poured a small amount of water into the basin to sponge her perspiring body and slip into a cool thin petticoat in hopes that she could rest easier.

A large moon emerged, full and white, to cast silver paths along the floor and cover the foliage and fields beyond with snowy whiteness. Charlotte gazed into the sky, only half seeing the clusters of stars twinkling in patches overhead.

She knew that Ben Tellison was somewhere on the Atlantic Ocean, on one of his ships, and sailing toward the Virginia shoreline. Was he thinking of her as often as she was picturing him in her mind? She thought about the approaching trip to the seaport and the meeting with the man she thought about every day since she left Tellison Hall.

"Lord," she whispered, "work out this meeting— whatever your will is for me. Help me to know the answer beyond all doubt and to accept whatever You have in mind for my life, without questioning Your wisdom.''

What Mr. Flaight felt or thought about the meeting, Charlotte couldn't determine, for she saw practically nothing of him, and when she did chance to pass him in the hallway, he met her glance with preoccupation. If the master were to be God's choice for her, then He would have to work out the miracles of salvation and love in the man's life. There could be no alternative.

When Charlotte rose early in the morning and walked across the carriage path to the kitchen, she was aware that the slaves were already at work in the fields. They trudged to the tobacco sections when the first streaks of dawn gave enough light to judge the plants ripe enough for swinging their sharp knives at the base of each. The rhythm was irregular but sure. The men placed the plants on the ground with the leaves carefully pointing in one specific direction and moved on to the next ones.

From the kitchen window, Charlotte watched the wary eyes of the master continually, tensely, search the heavens for dreaded signs of rain during harvest. Then as the day progressed, the sun beat unmercifully upon the harvest as well as the weary sweat-bathed bodies of the men, and he relaxed.

When Maryanne finished her breakfast and came to the kitchen, she and Charlotte went to Maryanne's room on the second floor. They spread a sheet on the floor and then let the heavy folds of satin drape on the covering while they worked on the seams of the satin skirt.

After an hour of working, Maryanne put her needle aside and said, ''Come on, Charlotte, let's walk out to the fields. We've seen very little of James and Papa since harvest began. Besides we need a rest from so much close work.'' Charlotte would have preferred finishing the seams, but she was eager to see, at close hand, what was happening in the fields.

169

The two followed the worm fence and then climbed on the top rung of the railing to sit and watch in the shade of an oak. They mopped the perspiration from their foreheads and glanced about.

Some of the slaves inspected and cut. Others carried the ripened, pliable, sun-drenched stalks, heaped in turns upon their shoulders, to the forked scaffoldings that were constructed strategically in mid sections located in the fields.

The muscles of the men rippled with the blows of the knives and with the lifting of the loads they carried.

"Papa never stops working," Maryanne sighed, "for the crop is so very demanding. If he were married and happy, perhaps he would give up these time-consuming efforts and simply raise corn, wheat, and sugar beets.

Charlotte studied the master, the steward, and the slaves carting the tobacco on drying poles from the field to the tobacco houses so the crop could dry under cover and in tiers. She doubted seriously that Mr. Flaight ever eased up on working or ever would. There was a great question in her mind whether he would even let up if he had a wife to care for him.

Periodically Maryanne waved to her betrothed and he, in turn, smiled and waved his hand in response.

"I'll be so happy to be married," she said. "We'll have the entire winter to be together and not have to worry about shipping hogsheads of tobacco to the warehouse all winter long. It's not worth it, I'll tell you frankly," she claimed defiantly. "Even when the tobacco reaches England, the market price is often lower than what it is here in America."

"Why does he continue to do it then?" asked Charlotte turning to study the serious girl beside her.

"Because he inherited great debts from his father and he tries to rid himself of them by sending more and better prize tobacco to try to erase more of the debts. Unfortunately, it is not working out that way. One day he'll realize that.''

Charlotte thought of the words of Mr. Tellison's captains. ''Spendthrifts.'' The word did not apply to Mr. Flaight nor probably to any other planter. Little did the English shippers know the agony behind those hogsheads they carried, in their holds, to the greedy merchants waiting to receive them.

One week before the banquet, Maryanne tried on her completed wedding dress before the huge mirror in the drawing room. The look of satisfaction and love spread across her face as she stared at the lovely image of herself.

''Just two weeks and I will be Mrs. James Blighton,'' she crooned happily.

Charlotte smiled. ''Where is the church in which you'll be married? In the village?''

''Oh, no. We'll not be married in the village church. Papa doesn't like the vicar and he doesn't like the church. We'll be married right here in the house. I'll walk down the central staircase, from my room here, and James will be waiting for me at the bottom step. Won't it be terribly romantic?'' breathed the happy girl.

Charlotte wondered how long the master would push God out of his life and try to carry the heavy load of debt and unbelief alone. The answer seemed so obvious to her. If he prayed about his problems, God would show him the answer.

''You will make a stunning bride, Maryanne,'' Charlotte assured the ecstatic girl.

''And you will too, Charlotte. Either for your Ben, or for Papa.''

While the tobacco dried in tiers in the tobacco houses, the slaves were sent to clear the new land.

171

From sunup to sundown the dull steady thud of the heavy headed poll exes echoed and reechoed as they bit into the timber to the west of the plantation. The men's muscles flexed and rippled on huge arms that axed and pummeled the timber until the darker bits gave way to white meat underneath and the whole crumbled and finally toppled to the ground. The slave women, children, and weaker old men were sent out to pile the brushwood, roots, and small pieces of timber into piles to be burned.

Two days before the banquet, the slaves were talking excitedly when Charlotte finished her rounds of inspecting the house. She was tired from a full day of working plus helping bake the special fruitcakes for the approaching wedding. Her busy mind paid little heed to the animated talk of the servants.

Charlotte was grateful that she had the wedding preparations to make her days sail by, and now it was two days before the appointed time to meet Ben Tellison at the seaport.

As soon as supper ended, Maryanne flew into the kitchen with, "Oh, Charlotte you are coming to the burning tonight, aren't you?"

For a moment Charlotte stared at the girl in dumb silence. "Burning?" she asked.

"Yes. Haven't you heard the slaves talking about it?"

"I really didn't pay much attention to what they were discussing," she admitted smiling. "I guess I've got the banquet on my mind right now."

"Well, you can't miss the burning tonight, that's all there is to it. Once a year the slaves gather to burn the brush piles that collect after the new land is cleared. The excitement and the singing is quite festive. Do say you'll come," pleaded Maryanne. "You can walk with Papa and James and me."

"How soon do you leave?"

"At sundown."

As soon as the slaves were able to finish their tasks as well as their supper, they began to emerge from their cabins and congregate on the carriage path at the rear of the house. The air was colder for a change. All were wrapped in whatever garments their abundance afforded against the chilling air of late September. They waited patiently. But there was an aura of excitement in their veins.

When Mr. Blighton and Maryanne appeared on the carriage path, they motioned for Charlotte to accompany them. The slaves fell in line behind them and they made their way across the edge of the fields following close by the zig zag worm fence all the way to the new ground where the first section of brush and small timber was ready to ignite.

The steward took his tinder box and strode over to the first brush pile. The anxious black faces watched until the thing caught fire and began to blaze. As the fury burst forth and flames leapt high into the blackness of night, their spirits, as well, gave way accordingly to great mirth. As one man led out in singing, the rest joined in the chanting and clapping until all swayed back and forth in time with the beat of the songs.

In the brightness, Charlotte watched the master approach. For awhile he stared vacantly into the fire without speaking. Then turning and facing her he asked, "Why do you stand so far away from the fire?"

"Fires don't excite me much after the tragedy of losing my family in one."

"I suppose not." He faced the fire once more and continued his vacant staring with lips tightly pursed.

Charlotte watched a happy Maryanne clinging to her James, in the light of the flames, but all the merriment couldn't blot out the desire to get away from the uncomfortable feeling and the memory of the last blaze she encountered. She started to move away.

"If you're going back to the house, I'll go with you," said Mr. Flaight.

"There's no need."

The master accompanied her to the house in spite of her objections. As they walked, Charlotte thought she felt his hand on her arm once when they came to some uneven ground.

"It's early," he stated. "Walk with me by the river before you go to your room."

The first stars of evening shown white and brilliant in their clear blue surroundings and a pale moon rose from the east to make black silhouettes of the branches. From the crepe myrtle bows, a cardinal sang its sleepy songs before closing its eyes for the night.

"We can have a double wedding along with Maryanne and James here at the house," the master said interrupting the silence of the evening.

"I can make no promises, sir."

"You have over six and a half years left on your conviction," he responded flatly. "I offer you a place as my wife. I could demand it."

"Yes, you could. But you won't."

"So you still think this man will want you? He will have to buy you back and he won't want to do that."

"I will know in two days if he does or not." she answered softly.

"And I say you're a fool to wait. He will not want you."

Charlotte bit her lip to stop an angry retort. "Surely," she said with a tight rein on her temper, "you'd not want me for a wife knowing I love another."

"I am not convinced that you do." His reply was calm and cynical. "I'll be waiting when he refuses to have you." With this, he turned and walked toward the house.

A tear slid silently to her cheek, making a zig zag path to her chin. She wasn't certain what the Lord had in store. She wouldn't know for sure until she stood before Ben Tellison on board ship and looked straight into his eyes for that answer.

The morning of the banquet dawned bright and clear and was unusually warm for the end of September, according to Annie. With much personal discipline on her part, Charlotte was able to keep her mind on her work. She did not see the master until it was nearly time to leave.

Quickly she bathed and put on her emerald gown. As she arranged her hair to perfection, with curls down the back of her neck, she wondered if Ben would find her changed. She was still slender but her proportions were fuller. Charlotte knew her color was excellent after spending more time in the sun than she ever had done before. Her cheeks were a blossoming pink and the brilliance in her eyes were the look of young love. The gown enhanced not only the color of her skin and shining wheat-colored hair, but also her face.

Maryanne slowly walked Charlotte to the doorway and informed her that she had done a little praying of her own, for she didn't want her friend to go back to England where she would never see her again. Charlotte embraced Maryanne and planted a kiss on her forehead.

"You forget that I am promised for six and a half years, for your father paid that amount for me. I may be back unless God works out other plans for me."

The two bade each other goodbye through tear-filled eyes, for the future was uncertain.

"There is always the possibility that God will yet give you to Papa," Maryanne said through her tears.

"If God wills it, I would accept it," answered Charlotte. "But I will know before long, won't I?"

"You will know, yes. Goodbye, Charlotte. I owe you so much that I can never repay."

"Ask God to make you a good wife if I don't see you again."

Maryanne nodded and walked with Charlotte down the path toward the boat landing. Charlotte wondered if she would walk this way again or if this would be the last time that she would stroll beneath the huge trees along the river.

Mr. Flaight and his steward were deep in conversation when they approached. Charlotte shifted her cloak from one arm to the other and waited by the path until the master looked over and saw her there. She studied the powerfully built man with his muscled arms folded across his chest. His lips were pressed tightly together in a pensive mood while he stared, through eyes squinting against the sun, toward the east. Charlotte decided that he was rather good looking in his well-fitted dark suit. It was the first time she had seen him dressed in something other than the coarse homespuns.

The sun was bright bringing out the gold in her hair. She knew that Mr. Flaight studied her but she kept her eyes away from him. She didn't want to give him any encouragement where she was concerned.

He walked to where Charlotte and his daughter waited by the path. If he noticed the tears in Maryanne's eyes and on her cheeks, he chose to ignore them. The look on his face seemed to say that it was a foolish waste of emotion, for Charlotte would be back; her former employer wouldn't want her. Mr. Flaight put out his hand to help Charlotte into the boat. When they were seated, he nodded to the slaves and the vessel began its route to the seaport.

For just a moment, he glanced back at his daughter waving a tearful farewell to her friend.

Charlotte turned to watch the estate gradually slip

from sight as the boat glided steadily down stream. So much had happened since she arrived in the spring. Her thoughts slipped back to the hostility that Mr. Flaight made no pretense of hiding when she first came to the plantation. Why, she wondered, did he want to marry her after that? Was he truly capable of showing love to a wife? What really was the situation that existed between him and his deceased wife?

For some distance the man simply stared out over the dark waters of the James River and said nothing to Charlotte. When he finally spoke he said, "You won't like going back onto a ship again."

"It isn't so bad when you know that you do not have to go on board as a prisoner."

"Mm. I'm sure you like the climate here better than you did the English temperatures. I understand that it is much colder there."

"With God's help I can be happy anywhere He places me." Charlotte answered without waivering.

The afternoon sun threw long purple shadows along the shore in shaded areas cooled by overhanging oaks and maples in varying degrees of green and amber hues. In different places along the way, she felt she remembered the vaguely familiar scene.

The same slaves who rowed her to the plantation five months earlier were now rowing her back to the same place in the bay—and to a waiting ship. The thought caused her heart to beat with anxiety and anticipation.

Charlotte caught her first glimpse of the tall masts of the barkentine that lay at rest in the harbor. The evening's sunset shone upon the folded sails, turning them from gray to pale pink. The patches of amber lapped and danced on little ripples of water hitting the sides of the ship. Charlotte gave a start and her voice caught within her throat.

"He's inside that vessel," she whispered to herself.

"Does he wait for me? Will he be kind – or stern?" And suddenly her mouth grew dry and she was apprehensive at the prospects of seeing Ben Tellison again.

Charlotte was unaware that Mr.Flaight studied her reactions carefully from his side of the boat.

After he climbed from the vessel, he reached down his hand to help her onto the wharf. He held onto her arm as they made their way across the long dock to the planks that led onto the huge Tellison ship.

"Many coaches were depositing gentleman planters and their ladies along the walkway. They made their way to the planking that connected the shore with the deck beyond where Tellison sailors waited to escort the guests below deck.

When Mr. Flaight stepped onto the top deck of the barkentine, he said, "You are, by law, still my possession, Charlotte. There are six and a half years left in the agreement and I have the bill of sale with me to prove it."

"I am well aware of that fact, sir."

Then the master looked at her before they reached the ladder to go below. "What is the name of the man you are to meet so I can talk with him?"

"Tellison."

For a moment the man stared at her in complete shock. "Tellison? Ben Tellison, the shipper, was your former employer?"

"Yes, sir," answered Charlotte while the cool evening breezes moved the curls about her neck ever so slightly.

Mr. Flaight said no more but took Charlotte's arm to help her down the ladder and to hold her gently, but firmly, as she lowered herself the last few rungs to the lower deck.

Anxiously Charlotte's eyes passed over the planters dressed in velvets, with hair powdered, and accompa-

178

nied by ladies in billowing silks. She began walking slowly toward the spacious captain's quarters where talk and laughter filled the room and spilled out into the larger passage. Tables and chairs lined the areas along the ship's sides and sailors heaped platters of food on the linen cloths.

Charlotte was standing still and glancing toward the doorway when she saw him. For one breathtaking moment her heart stood still. It was as if the blood in her veins no longer wanted to flow.

He was dressed in black silk but his hair was not powdered as the fashion was. When Ben's eyes beheld Charlotte, he stopped in the middle of his conversation and started toward her.

She watched him move forward while he breathed her name. "Charlotte." She heard Mr. Flaight draw in his breath as Ben reached out and took both of her hands in his. "Oh, Charlotte," he said. "You don't know how anxious I've been about you."

"Mr. Tellison," Charlotte said softly. "This is my present master, Mr. Flaight. Mr. Tellison."

The two men acknowledged each other's presence with a nod while studying one another. Mr. Tellison was the first to speak. "Yes. Mr. Flaight and I are acquainted. It's his prized sweet scented tobacco that gives his plantation its good name."

Then turning toward Charlotte, he smiled that uneven crooked smile that she remembered so well— the smile with one corner of his mouth curving upward prior to the other side following in a moment or two.

"You're looking more beautiful than ever, Charlotte," he added, totally ignoring the master beside her. She felt a slight color rise and looked down before he continued, his eyes never leaving her face for an instant. Then his expression became somber as he spoke softly.

"I'm sorry, Charlotte, about all of this. The lieutenant told me everything. I had searched everywhere for you and found no trace of you. He's on my ships now as an officer. But I have something for you to make amends in some small way." And he reached into his pocket while he studied the girl's face before handing her a letter.

"Your full pardon, Charlotte. You're free again. My mother confessed to the deed before she died," he whispered. "She admitted that she deceitfully did this to you."

Charlotte reached slowly for the letter and stared into the face of the man she had thought about so often in the past months. "Free, sir? I'm no longer a convict?" Truly these were wonderful words to her ears—like spring that comes suddenly on the rim of bitter winter blasts.

Mr. Tellison continued to look into the girl's eyes and then, putting his hand on hers, said "After I pay Mr. Flaight back the price he paid for you, I want you to accompany me for a little stroll on the top deck. I have something to ask you."

Charlotte clasped the letter to her heart while tears slid down her cheeks. She barely saw the business transaction that transpired between the two men, the business that paid her pardon in full. The tears in her eyes blotted out most of it.

"Thank you, Lord," she whispered under her breath. "Thank you for your great mercy in delivering me from this bitter humiliation."

"Now, sir," Ben said to Mr. Flaight, "please help yourself to the food. If you will excuse me, I have some unfinished business to attend to with Charlotte." And before she could say a word, he took hold of her arm and helped her up the narrow stairway to the upper deck. Then pulling her behind the mizzen-mast, and out of the view of prying eyes, he whispered, "Charlotte, have you missed me as much as I have missed you?"

"Oh, yes—yes, I have," she breathed huskily.

"When I left Tellison Hall for a few days last February, I went to London to cancel my shipping contract with the government. I probably wouldn't have gone as soon as I did, but my conscience gave me no peace—not after you came to the house." Here Ben put his hands behind his back and stared out over the bay. "You see, I shipped convicts to the colonies, Charlotte. The rival company's ship is the one you sailed on."

"The lieutenant told you."

"Yes. He told me. I could learn nothing from the servants at the house, for my mother threatened to get rid of any who told me what happened to you. Naturally, I suspected something, for the one little maid burst into tears every time I talked to her. It wasn't until Lieutenant Drummond returned on one of my ships that I learned the truth. He came to me and told me the details of your conviction and sentence and told me, also, who you were with here in the colony. It seems Drummond has friends in the seaport here— friends who were willing to get the information about you before he left port." Then turning back to Charlotte he said, "I have lived in an agony that some master was mistreating you—beating you, perhaps. I prayed for you constantly. But tell me, were you treated well?"

"Yes, I was treated well."

"And what of the convict ship. Was it horrible?"

"It's in the past. Please don't worry about it; I put the whole thing out of my mind long ago."

"I have prayed for you constantly, Charlotte— prayed that you would be treated well and that you would be happy to see me in spite of all that happened as a result of living in my house."

Ben placed his warm hands on her shoulders. "Did Mr. Flaight ask you to marry him?"

"Yes, but I couldn't do it."

"He had much to offer a wife. What kept you from accepting, Charlotte?"

"You did," she whispered as the sun sank below the wilderness to the west and silhouetted them against the night sky.

"Tell me," he said when his lips moved away from hers long enough to ask another question, "do you like it here in Virginia?"

"Yes. I have learned to like the climate very much."

"I'm pleased to hear it, my love, for I plan to settle here and start a shipping business from this port. Will you marry me and spend your life with me here? Neither of us has anything to draw us back to England, do we?"

"No, Ben, nothing. But I could be happy anywhere you were with me."

"I was trusting God that you would agree," he said with a pleased chuckle coming from deep in his throat. "I have already talked to the vicar in the church here in Williamsburg, and he will perform the wedding tomorrow morning." And when Ben gathered Charlotte in his arms once more, he silently kissed away the salty drops that spilled rapidly from her eyes and made little streaks down to her chin.

ABOUT THE AUTHOR

JEANNE CHEYNEY is a former teacher and librarian who now spends much of her time writing and illustrating educational books with her husband. She enjoys raising quail, making puppets, and painting with water colors in addition to writing. The author of two books, this is her first Serenade Saga.

A Letter To Our Readers

Dear Reader:

In order that we might better contribute to your reading enjoyment, we would appreciate your taking a few minutes to respond to the following questions and return to:

Editor, Serenade Books
The Zondervan Publishing House
1415 Lake Drive, S.E.
Grand Rapids, Michigan 49506

1. Did you enjoy reading THE CONVICTION OF CHARLOTTE GREY?

   ☐ Very much. I would like to see more books by this author!
   ☐ Moderately
   ☐ I would have enjoyed it more if _____

2. Where did you purchase this book? _____

3. What influenced your decision to purchase this book?

   ☐ Cover   ☐ Back cover copy
   ☐ Title   ☐ Friends
   ☐ Publicity   ☐ Other _____

4. Would you be interested in reading other Serenade/ Serenata or Serenade/Saga Books?

   ☐ Very interested
   ☐ Moderately interested
   ☐ Not interested

5. Please indicate your age range:

   ☐ Under 18   ☐ 25–34   ☐ 46–55
   ☐ 18–24   ☐ 35–45   ☐ Over 55

6. Would you be interested in a Serenade book club? If so, please give us your name and address:

   Name _____

   Occupation _____

   Address _____

   City _____ State _____ Zip _____

Serenade Saga books are inspirational romances in historical settings, designed to bring you a joyful, heart-lifting reading experience.

Serenade Saga books available in your local book store:

#1 SUMMER SNOW, Sandy Dengler
#2 CALL HER BLESSED, Jeanette Gilge
#3 INA, Karen Baker Kletzing
#4 JULIANA OF CLOVER HILL,
     Brenda Knight Graham
#5 SONG OF THE NEREIDS, Sandy Dengler
#6 ANNA'S ROCKING CHAIR,
     Elaine Watson
#7 IN LOVE'S OWN TIME,
     Susan C. Feldhake
#8 YANKEE BRIDE, Jane Peart
#9 LIGHT OF MY HEART, Kathleen Karr
#10 LOVE BEYOND SURRENDER,
     Susan C. Feldhake
#11 ALL THE DAYS AFTER SUNDAY,
     Jeanette Gilge
#12 WINTERSPRING, Sandy Dengler
#13 HAND ME DOWN THE DAWN,
     Mary Harwell Sayler
#14 REBEL BRIDE, Jane Peart
#15 SPEAK SOFTLY, LOVE, Kathleen Yapp
#16 FROM THIS DAY FORWARD, Kathleen Karr
#17 THE RIVER BETWEEN, Jacquelyn Cook
#18 VALIANT BRIDE, Jane Peart
#19 WAIT FOR THE SUN, Maryn Langer
#20 KINCAID OF CRIPPLE CREEK, Peggy Darty
#21 LOVE'S GENTLE JOURNEY, Kay Cornelius
#22 APPLEGATE LANDING, Jean Conrad

Serenade Serenata books are inspirational romances in contemporary settings, designed to bring you a joyful, heart-lifting reading experience.

Serenade Serenata books available in your local bookstore:

#22 THROUGH A GLASS DARKLY,
   Sara Mitchell

Watch for other books in both the *Serenade Saga* (historical) and *Serenade Serenata* (contemporary) series coming soon.